THE JUSTICE BRIGADE

THE JUSTICE BRIGADE

A Montana Story

Manshadow Waylett

authorHOUSE®

AuthorHouse™ LLC
1663 Liberty Drive
Bloomington, IN 47403
www.authorhouse.com
Phone: 1-800-839-8640

Old Montana Prison taken from Wikipedia:
Author:Tanankyo

http://en.wikipedia.org/wiki/File:CB1OMP.jpg

Published by AuthorHouse 07/25/2014

ISBN: 978-1-4918-9952-6 (sc)
ISBN: 978-1-4918-9951-9 (e)

DEDICATION

The Justice Brigade is a fictional novel that weaves the rule of old Montana vigilante justice into a modern setting. Without structured law and order, people in the early days sought justice in ways that many of us would like to return to today. The fictional vigilante order of this story is set into present-day law enforcement in Montana and nearby areas where their clandestine work is determined to make sure that law and order and justice are kept in balance.

This story is dedicated to law and order, in deep gratitude for efforts of those brave and determined men and women whose commitments to justice have built and preserved it for the good citizens of Montana from its origins to the present.

ACKNOWLEDGMENT

This story would not have come to you without the encouragement, enthusiasm and interest so abundantly given to its preparation and completion by Marlene, Audrey, our mother, Frances, Leisa and my magnificent parents-in-law in Texas.

Of special significance is the historical perspective of the color, excitement, and richness of our Montana family heritage, passed to us in the stories of our Waylett pioneer ancestors. No one could have given them more vivid treatment to it than our grandfather, Bert, or our dad, Joe.

Not to be overlooked are the many old timers whose experiences and tales gave depth to my youthful years in Montana. They were prospectors, miners, cowboys, farmers, loggers, railroaders, Indians, barkeeps, merchants and lawmen. The wisdom of one particular retired officer of the highway patrol was an inspiration for this story. His thesis about law and order was that the two sometimes become separated.

He cautioned that with our laws becoming more complex and trials becoming more liberal, the system of law and order could sometimes betray our sense of true justice. In those instances, he concluded that people would always seek justice and overcome the failures of the system.

This story is gratefully dedicated to memories of the colorful old folks who gave us treasured guidance. Let this be a tribute to the untiring efforts of those brave and determined men and women in law enforcement who have preserved the virtues of justice for the good citizens of Montana from the pioneer days of our state to the present.

Montana Highway Patrol patch.

The Montana Highway Patrol was created in 1936. In 1956, Chief Alex B. Stephenson added "3-7-77" as a tribute to the Vigilantes.

PART I

Knock On Stone

CHAPTER 1

The Return of Eddie Weeks

As the Rocky Mountain Stage Lines cruiser slowed into the down ramp off Interstate 90 to enter Superior, Montana, Edward Weeks was on his feet to retrieve his parcel of belongings from the overhead rack. The arrival in his hometown had taken only two hours from Spokane to the west but it had been a long journey since his release and parole from Walla Walla State Penitentiary in Washington. Edward had served only eight years of a fourteen-year sentence for imprisoning and molesting two little girls, aged eight and nine. The granting of a furlough to visit an elderly and seriously ailing mother in the small Montana lumbering town had been a difficult argument with his parole officer. As her only child, Edward managed to convince him of the need for compassion in allowing what could be a final visit to her, and the board officials agreed.

With a grinding of gears, the creaking of suspension and applied brakes, the bus came to a stop at Marshall's Service and Travel Stop. As the door hissed closed behind him, Edward was the only passenger to step onto the pavement into the quiet of a clear mountain evening. He was thirsty for a soft drink and wanted a snack before walking to the hospital to see his mother. As he started toward the entrance, someone quietly called to him from the shadows beside the store where a car was parked.

"Hey Eddie, over here!" called Mineral Sheriff Deputy Carl "Chub" Denton. "I see you finally made it back to our little town, and I'm sorry to hear that your mom isn't doing well." As he hesitantly walked closer, Edward could see the roof lights and black and white markings of the police cruiser. "Oh yeah, hi Chub! Well, I am only back for a couple of weeks, so this may be the last time I get to see her. I suppose my P.O. in Walla Walla had to call and tell you I was coming."

"Right Eddie, would you mind sitting here in the car with me so that we can talk? I have a couple of things to go over with you. Right here, plenty of room in the back seat."

Denton held the door open as he approached and Edward placed his parcel inside as he cautiously seated himself. "Sorry, Eddie, but department policy says that no one can bring things into the passenger compartment, so I will have to hang on to that little bag of yours while we chat." He removed the parcel as he spoke and casually tossed it into the front seat. Edward felt a chill and slightly shuddered as the deputy closed the door behind him.

Speaking now from the front seat through the steel mesh that separated the front from the rear compartments, Denton continued, "Well, we have a minor matter to clear up that may briefly delay your visit but shouldn't be much of a problem to you. Of course, you remember my investigation of that little girl who was killed here about nine years ago? You know, the seven-year-old who was raped, beaten and left to decompose out near Haugen. She is the one I asked you so many questions about, but we never were able to conclude that case. It was just a simple lack of good evidence."

"Yes, I remember you grinding me away on that one, but I did nothing to that kid, and you had no proof I did. So what's the problem now?"

"Well, Eddie, no real problem, but I have been asked to arrange transport for you over to Scribner to look at some evidence the State Crime Lab has stored there to see if you can give us some help on it. A couple of state detectives will probably want to talk to you. It won't take much time at all, and we will bring you right back here early as tomorrow. Hate like hell to interrupt this visit, but you know how it is with unsolved crimes; they just never seem to go away."

"Hey look, Chub, this isn't the right time for me to be doing anything with you guys when my mom might pass on at any moment. For shit's sake, don't you have any care that my mom is dying here? Can't you wait on this for a couple of days until I have at least seen her and given her some comfort? Goddamn it, you guys haunt someone like a bunch of stinkin' vultures!"

By now the deputy had the cruiser moving toward the entrance ramp to Interstate 90 heading eastward. "Sorry, guy. This is out of my hands and I just have to go along with the program. Make yourself comfortable and we will get you taken care of as soon as possible." With that, Denton picked up the cruiser's radio microphone and keyed it for a call to his dispatcher. "Hello Mary, patch me over to State Patrol please." Within a minute after a muffled acknowledgement, a clear male voice responded over the speaker.

"Hello Chub, Mike here. What do you need buddy?"

"Hey Mike, that was quick. What's your ten-twenty? I have a special Jim Bridger request for you tonight. Can you meet me outside of Scribner?

"Sure Chub. I am already westbound on 90 out of Alberton, and if you are leaving town, how about meeting me at the rest stop?"

"Ten-four buddy, about ten minutes. See you there."

As the darkness closed along the highway, Edward leaned back in the hard, black vinyl seat to ease the tension gripping his entire body, but there was no relief. He was a prisoner again and this one had a foul and terrifying feel to it, a fear worse than he had ever known. This time no one but he and Deputy Denton was aware of where he was or where he was going.

The old Montana Territorial Prison, built in 1869, stands as tall and ominous as a red granite cliff in the center of the town of Scribner, Van Blaricom County, Montana. In its years of service to law and order, it had earned a nation-wide reputation for harshness, discomfort and stone-hard lock-down from which there was no escape. It is now a state historical landmark and remains partially in penal service as the Van Blaricom County jail.

The territorial prison, having seen Montana grow from a wild and struggling territory into modern statehood, outgrew its capacity in mid-life but remained the principal detention facility for hardened criminals until a new maximum security prison was completed. In 1979, the old prison was given to tiny, rural Van Blaricom County, and Sheriff Tom Davis began the conversion of its main cellblocks into a jail that would be large enough to serve the county's needs for possibly the next century. As budgeting permitted, he was able to rent jail space in the renovated premises to other counties whose facilities were over-crowed, and thereby return a measure of profit to the Van Blaricom County coffers. The practice has been successfully continued over the years, earning Van Blaricom County high visibility and prestige among law enforcement officials throughout the state.

In carrying out the many renovations begun by Davis, the county also adopted plans for the future use of part of the prison as a museum. Succeeding sheriffs were meagerly budgeted to build a secured, segregated area for that purpose, but no completion date was prescribed. Initial construction efforts managed to close off such a facility within the walls, featuring a separate entrance that would house the maintenance staff, janitors and workshops until it could be converted into a museum. The modified facility provided the only access to the basement of the old prison known as "The Dungeon," an area of some 60 "holes" or isolation cells, which was once used to contain and punish the most violent prisoners. Each was cased with sheet steel covering solid stone walls, six feet wide by six feet high by eight feet deep.

CHAPTER 2

The Little Gold Ring

In a 1989 speech in the Scribner High School auditorium, Governor Harold D. Smith commemorated the tenth anniversary of the opening of the new prison by recounting highlights in the history of Montana law and order. He illuminated the early days of the Territorial Prison and the brave and tireless efforts of the vigilantes, saying, "In the midst of wanton banditry and murder, those noble warriors of peace and decency were the first to bring civility, justice and safety to the earliest, most God-fearing citizens of our state. Thank Almighty God their spirit and dedication still survives."

After describing the substantial growth of the state's new penal facilities, in which he boasted a major role, he added a curious commentary about a "vigilante code" that continues to serve Montana's concepts of justice and the treatment of its criminals. "I especially want to recognize that small group of stalwart officers of our courts who quietly bonded together to systematically cleanse our state of its most heinous and destructive felons." In another address later in the afternoon, he emotionally praised the many achievements of state, county and local lawmen, and prosecutors from across the state at the annual conclave of the Montana Vigilance Association (MVA) in Scribner.

From there, Governor Smith was escorted to a small conference room in the nearby Biedler Corral Motel to socialize and enjoy cocktails with the selected few members of the MVA who were part of an elite group named the Justice Brigade. The origins of this society are as clouded as the estimates of its membership, the purposes they serve, numbers of committees involved, or the locations of any of their officials. The organization may have been formed in recent times or it may be a continuation of the original vigilantes whose operations were never officially closed. Its membership comes from the MVA, and their induction into the Justice Brigade is a high form of recognition awarded to individuals who have earned it by outstanding performance in their jobs.

The public is aware that, in order to be chosen, the inductees must be exemplary citizens of high principles and dedicated to their professions. However the organization's work is not visible to them in any form of lawmaking or law enforcement even though it has had a discreet, firm impact on those areas. When admitted into this exclusive society, new members are awarded a small, Montana native gold pinkie ring bearing a Montana Yogo sapphire centered between the letters, "J" and "B". Over the years, many wealthy benefactors have endowed substantial amounts of money to the Justice Brigade although its actual wealth and banking sources are unknown.

As the governor conversed with Justice Brigade men and women clustered around him, he was introduced to the new members, who had just taken a solemn oath of allegiance to the Brigade, as they were summoned into private briefings by its senior members.

The oath of Brigade membership is one of the most solemn and rigid commitments that anyone could ever make as an officer of the courts. Before the pledge of loyalty is sworn, the individual is allowed an opportunity to decline because the oath carries with it the understanding that any compromise of Justice Brigade secrecy could result in a charge of treachery. Those who accept the appointment are given a stern, verbal briefing by other members on the organization's protocols, rules, and methods of communications. No notes are allowed and the most important item to be accurately memorized is the "800" number which is used only for two-way operational communication. Its location and details of its management are secretly maintained, excepting for records that ultimately come into the hands of the Council of Ten where all decisions are made and handed down.

The Justice Brigade accepts only five new members each year, and no one may be admitted unless they are at least a second-generation Montanan and are nominated by at least three other members. An executive board known as the Council of Ten makes final approval of the five nominees and inductions are handled by a senior member of the organization at large. Strangely, there are no written membership rolls of the Brigade and no meeting minutes are kept. No single member has any idea of the dimension of the organization, and those seated as the Council of Ten are known only to each other.

Over the years, the Justice Brigade has accepted men and women from all elements of the legal system; elected officials, judges, legislators, prosecutors, trial attorneys, and federal, state and local law enforcement officers. It is rumored that a couple of Montana governors have been members of the organization.

CHAPTER 3
Last Flight to Big Fork

Two years before the most recent MVA and Justice Brigade convention, one of the most publicized murder trials in U.S. history had concluded with the exoneration of the accused, Jerry P. (Jeep) Rogers. Its parallel to the earlier O.J. Simpson debacle, known as the trial of the century, could not have been more vivid.

Rogers was a renowned Afro-American professional baseball star, private pilot, leader of a regional Black Moslem religious order, magazine publisher and wealthy, international playboy. He had twice been divorced and was legally separated from his third wife Annette and her two children of a former marriage. Jeep and Annette resided in separate town homes in the most elite section of the Chicago suburbs. Their pending divorce had been through major complications over the course of two years, primarily involving disputes over his behavior during the marriage, abuse of his wife and her children and, naturally, assets and alimony.

At a point in time, Annette and her children were found bludgeoned to death in their home and Jeep Rogers was arrested and charged with the crimes. The accusation brought the worldwide press into a feeding frenzy, saturating viewers and readers with daily, global coverage of every investigative lead, rumor and slightest suspicion surrounding the case. Through weeks of trial preparation, the weight of evidence seemed insurmountable for his defense, even though Rogers had employed the most expensive, competent team of criminal lawyers available. Prosecutors were more than confident about winning with the mountains of physical and scientific evidence they had accumulated. His attorneys rebutted each statement by displaying their own arrogance over an easy defeat of it all in court.

Although Jeep Rogers was not allowed bond at his initial arraignment, his lawyers continued to argue for a dollar amount so that he could be free to visit and care for an aged father who was residing in a Toledo rest home. Two weeks prior to trial date, the presiding judge set bail at $1.5 million, which was immediately posted and Rogers was released under tight restrictions to attend to his father. Within days, Rogers came up missing along with his twin-jet Lotus Star luxury aircraft, and one of the largest, nationwide manhunts in history ensued. Four days later, Rogers was captured in Sierra Vista, Arizona, and returned to Chicago for trial. While his father lay dying, he had made a vain attempt to cross the border into Mexico, carrying a horde of cash and valuables. By the time he was returned to the custody of the court, his father had passed on.

Jeep made no effort to attend his father's funeral and sent only a modest spray of flowers with a card that simply said, "In the memory of dear old Dad".

As the trial date neared, jury selection was completed with a make up of nine Afro-Americans, two Caucasians and one Asian American. The four alternate jurors were all Afro-Americans and eleven of the sixteen members of the jury were females. The televised trial of Rogers went on for weeks, overshadowing most other news events. Rogers' team propagandized publicly and battered every prosecution witness with slurs, innuendoes and accusations of racial bias. Racism was amplified in every element of their defense. At the end, the jury found Rogers not guilty. The verdict, added to that of the Simpson case, created global outrage and caused a schism in U.S. race relations between black and white that may never be repaired.

For several months, Rogers kept a low profile while trying to maintain his international playboy lifestyle. He was occasionally spotted frolicking in a posh resort area or casino by the "paparazzi", in the company of some glamorous showgirl or celebrity prostitute. Otherwise, he was working to reinvest his substantial fortunes into more obscure but enviable living conditions where he could have the benefits of a pasha's mansion and the privacy of a remote wilderness retreat. After having his investment counselors assess hundreds of real estate possibilities around the planet, one choice loomed above all others. Big Fork, Montana, seemed to be the one place made to order for his purposes, as well as those of many other wealthy luminaries who had informally made Big Fork the Riviera of Montana.

Rogers' "people" had discreetly been working with a Big Fork real estate agent to identify a property that would meet a wide range of specifications which seemed to all be embodied in an exclusive estate owned by the CEO of a Japanese electronics company. Negotiations succeeded in arriving at a reasonable price that would require the approval of Rogers before the transaction was completed. The local brokerage reported to the Big Fork Chief of Police that Rogers would be flying into Whitefish International Airport in his own airplane and would require substantial security and protection measures. He planned to stay for two weeks to close on the property, tour the locality, and enjoy several days of fishing on Flathead Lake, and would be traveling around on his own in a private rental car.

In all events, Rogers insisted on complete secrecy for the visit, especially excluding the press.

Big Fork Chief of Police, Hal Riggs, was notified of Rogers' agenda a week prior to his arrival and immediately set about to scheduling his limited resources to covering all aspects of required secrecy and security. Riggs appointed Constable Reamy Nelson, youngest JB member, as principal body-guard and project coordinator, giving him discretion to define and employ whatever resources might be needed.

The same evening, Nelson made a phone call from a public phone to an 800 number on which he left a message about the coming visit of Rogers. Three days later, on his office telephone, he picked up to hear a deeply voiced caller that cryptically instructed, "Greetings brother, please meet with our Montana highway patrolman at Brushy Cove Coffee Stop at 3:45 P.M. regarding your visitor. Thank you Reamy."

A brilliant, sparkling Montana afternoon glistened from the fuselage of the tiny, silver and blue Lotus Star as it touched down on the single runway of the White Fish airport. In a few minutes the craft was guided to its tie down where a small group of people awaited their visitor to deplane. After gathering a few of his belongings inside, Rogers emerged alone, smiling and shaking hands with Chief Riggs and three real estate executives before being introduced to Nelson. As soon as the remainder of his cargo was loaded into his rented Grand Cherokee, a small convoy formed to escort him to Scott's Villa, one of the most exclusive apartment/condo complexes in the West.

Through cocktails and a light buffet lunch, Rogers was briefed on the roles of people there to assist him, most of which he courteously dismissed, insisting on being able to relax and freely explore things on his own. The only exception was that he wanted officer Reamy Nelson to accompany him wherever he went. He was very pleased about the absence of the press and curiosity seekers, as well as the obvious care everyone had taken to ensure his privacy.

Nelson spent three pleasant days in the company of Rogers, responding to his jokes, his wonderment at the grandeur surrounding the estate he was about to purchase and his enchantment with the calm, low-key atmosphere of Big Fork. They were on a first name basis as they ventured unnoticed around the community, golf courses, fishing facilities and nightclubs, Rogers driving the Cherokee and Nelson following in his unmarked police cruiser.

On the afternoon of the third day, Nelson suggested that Rogers might want to make a "special" acquaintance over cocktails with a sexy, young and wealthy widow who owned a fishing resort on the lake. Rogers responded immediately. Nelson arranged to meet him at 7:00 that evening, drive him to her place in the cruiser and handle the introductory formalities before leaving them alone. Rogers was delighted by the prospects and eager to make an appointment that Nelson had confidence would not be discussed with anyone at the Villa.

At precisely 6:18 P.M. Nelson pulled his cruiser into Jim's Truck Stop, the contract filling station for police vehicles. After topping off his tank and checking the oil, he made a point to chat with the owner about the latest lake fishing reports and lies that were always circulating at Jim's. He left at 6:22, remarking to Jim that he was able to make a late dinner with his wife and kids for a change. A hasty drive brought him into the visitor parking area of Scott's

Villa by 6:48, and he was on his way to the main lobby when he was met halfway by a beaming Jeep Rogers. Making small talk, they shuffled to the cruiser and were on the way south along the lakeshore at 6:53.

At exactly 7:00 P.M. Nelson noticed the flashing of police lights in his rear view mirror and he immediately pulled into the deserted Crystal Bay Rest Area, commenting to Rogers about how curious it was that they were being stopped by the highway patrol. As the patrolman approached, Nelson calmed Rogers' nervous looks by assuring him that it was obviously police business and that the patrolman was a personal friend of his. The officer approached and Nelson met him outside his vehicle, leaving the door open. As Rogers waited in the passenger seat, he was unable to hear the muffled dialogue between the two officers and was soon greeted by the patrolman.

"Hello Mr. Rogers, I'm Patrolman Davis. Sure sorry to interrupt your evening, sir, but I have been asked to detain you for a while. I followed along to meet you here rather than create any kind of scene back there in town and hope you don't mind."

"Yes, I'm Jeep Rogers and I want to know what in hell this is all about! I haven't done anything to be detained for, officer. This is my first trip ever to Montana, and the guy I am riding with here is a Big Fork police officer."

Davis approached the open door. As he leaned into the driver's side of the cruiser, he calmly and carefully explained, "Yes, I am sorry about all of this and I have known Nelson here for many years. It seems that the IRS has come up with something they want to talk to you about, and they asked us to bring you to Missoula for some questions. You aren't under arrest or anything, and they have made very comfortable hotel reservations for you there. I just have to ask you to come along with me, and I will be happy to bring you back to the villa tomorrow afternoon."

Outraged, Rogers fired back, "Bullshit! I'm not going anywhere until I talk to my lawyer and that will take some time for me to find him. The IRS can go straight to hell or come to see me themselves."

Davis replied in a low voice, "Look, I know how you must feel about this but I have no alternatives, just my orders. Tell you what. I will personally assure you that the IRS will not mistreat, harass or detain you for anything longer than the two hours of questions they promised. I don't like dealing with them any more than you do, sir, so please give me a break and cooperate. Just take a drive with me down to Missoula. We can make a pleasant trip out of it, and you will be back here tomorrow."

"Okay," said Rogers. "I guess I have no alternatives either but this really pisses me off! Probably the best thing is not to create another mess since I intend to live up here, but I will tell you for sure that I am being hassled and intend to sue to get them off my ass!"

Rogers then turned to the side in the cruiser, motioning to Nelson, "Hey Reamy, sorry about being distracted from that date you set up, so clear it with the little lady. Rain check for sure, huh? And soon!"

Nelson mumbled an affirmative comment and approached the passenger door to help Rogers out of the cruiser. At that point, Patrolman Davis apologized to Rogers for having to seat him in the rear compartment of his cruiser, saying, "I regret this but it's department policy, and I can do nothing about that for sure."

As Nelson seated himself behind the wheel of the unmarked cruiser, he watched the patrol car exit the rest station on the highway south to Missoula. He was but two minutes from his rural cottage and dinner with his little family. The time was 7:05 P.M.

The following morning at 9:00 A.M., Nelson made a telephone call to Chief Riggs from the lobby of Scott's Villa, to report that he had not heard from Rogers and had come by the villa to check on him. "He seems to have vanished, Chief. His Cherokee is here in the parking lot, but no one has seen him all night or this morning and he rarely misses breakfast. I saw him last when I left here at about 6:30 yesterday and went right home for dinner after filling up at Jim's. He said he would give me a call this morning, and I don't quite know what to make of this situation."

"Come on in to the station, Reamy," said Riggs. "He may have gotten the attention of some little skirt who took him home with her, maybe out jogging or playing golf. Who knows? But one thing for sure, we haven't put together a contingency plan for anything where he might really come up missing. Leave word for the Villa to call here when he shows up and let's you and I get together to work something out."

Nelson hung up the phone, a faint smirk playing on his lips as he glanced at the gold and sapphire ring on his right little finger.

CHAPTER 4

New Addition to the Old Prison

Janet Rivers, 53 year old divorcee, had finished a long day driving her mini-van from her home in Helena to remote Scribner, to cover the escape of three prisoners who had walked away from the institution's work farm. With origins in Chicago and 22 years as a reporter for the *Chicago Daily Horizon*, Rivers had earned national distinction as a conservative spokesperson and syndicated columnist on crime, law and order, and politics. In the ten years of her residency in Montana, she had become a popular figure wherever she went, a welcomed presence in any sheriff's office and most city or town police headquarters in the state. As well, she had fully integrated herself with an array of friends and social contacts among judges, state and local prosecutors, and legislators.

One of Rivers' closest contacts, rumored to be somewhat more than just a "friend," was Charles Gettys, FBI Special Agent in Helena. Gettys reported to FBI headquarters in Butte, known to be the Bureau's penal colony for wayward, error prone or otherwise semi-misfit agents who needed a sort of "purgatory" period before rejoining the popular ranks of the establishment. He always resented the dark stigma surrounding the workers in the Butte office because he had excelled in all categories of his 20 years with the Bureau for the sole purpose of acquiring a Montana assignment, the place of his birth. Nothing negative could be found in his fitness reports. All considered, Gettys was expected to soon be promoted to Special Agent in Charge, Butte regional headquarters.

Darkness had begun to settle into Scribner as Janet left 4-B's Restaurant, and she paused to watch the crimson and pink sunset cast a purple halo over the nearby Pintlar Mountains. Her long day and a late, filling steak dinner brought on a sweeping surge of exhaustion and drowsiness. The prison authorities, having pursued the escapees from dawn to dark, had developed several leads on their whereabouts but were unable to recapture them. Additional forces from all available law enforcement would be added the next morning, and the entire night would be devoted to pouring over all possible options, strategizing and planning the next layer of operations.

As she walked toward her parked van, Janet pondered her options. She could join the group's tactical conference for the remainder of the night, drive back to Helena and return the following morning to resume her coverage or get some rest in Scribner, freshen up and stay in contact.

By the time she had her van in motion, Janet had taken her third choice and was seeking a quiet place in town in which to park, lie down on the couch in the rear, and catch a few hours of sleep. The back street intersecting

Main, behind the Old Territorial Prison, seemed to be the most likely place at hand. She parked across the street from the rear entrance of the prison, locked the van doors, unfolded a fleece robe and settled into a comfortable position on the couch. Within a few minutes, she was sound asleep.

At some point an hour or so later, Janet was aroused from sleep by shouted orders and cursing coming from close by the van. Rising to peer out the side window, she saw a highway patrol car parked across the street and could see several figures moving about under the single lamp that illuminated the back entrance to the prison. Two men, armed with shotguns, were assisting a uniformed officer to forcibly extricate someone from the back seat of the cruiser, shove him over its rear deck and handcuff him. The prisoner was strenuously resisting, shouting and cursing as he was being moved through the open door into the courtyard of the old prison.

Janet gasped and shuddered as a shock of instant recognition struck her. The man being taken into the prison was no other than Jerry P. "Jeep" Rogers, Chicago baseball star and notorious freed killer! He had been her athletic idol years before and was the same to everyone in the Midwest. There was absolutely no mistake about it, Jeep Rogers was being jailed in the old prison, and she was going to immediately find out why. As she stirred around to get herself in order, the highway patrol car pulled away. By the time she was outside the van, the heavy back door of the prison was closed and locked and there was no sound or evidence of any disturbance to the quiet summer night in Scribner.

The scene was so vivid yet inconceivable in this remote part of Montana that, for an instant, Janet felt it might all have been an illusion . . . a dream extension to a long and intense day. The perplexing images of what she had witnessed kept sleep away from her most of the night. Surely tomorrow she would get to the truth of the matter. It had to have a rational explanation, and the people she knew in law enforcement would give her the answers. It just had to be something simple and reasonable.

CHAPTER 5

Room With No View

Jeep Rogers' anxieties had grown steadily more intense during the two and a half-hour drive with Patrolman Davis, and he reiterated his rage over and again about IRS harassment.

"Look, officer, I know this is boring the hell out of you, but I have to vent my anger over this whole racist maneuver by the IRS. I cannot understand why they couldn't be decent enough to get off their asses in Missoula, get into their taxpayer cars and come out to talk to me in person. This is purely a means of trying to embarrass and harass me with a bogus interview. I haven't done anything wrong with my taxes, and I have a flotilla of high-paid accountants to prove it!"

"Well, Jeep", said Davis, "I'm sure you will have your answers in a few minutes. Here we are in town, nearly at our destination, and everything will be cleared up soon."

"Sheeeiit, Davis! I thought Missoula was a bigger place than this. Damn! This is just a little dinky town, and I didn't see any highway sign for the place. Where is that big airport I took a nav beacon on out of Salt Lake City?"

The cruiser slowed southbound on Main Street and passed the main entrance and the long wall of the Old Territorial Prison. Patrolman Davis made a right turn onto the first intersection behind the prison and eased to a stop beneath a small shaded light over an open doorway to the courtyard, where two men with shotguns stood idly waiting for them. Paying little notice to the darkened mini-van parked across the street, Davis slid out of the cruiser and opened the passenger door, asking Jeep to come with him to meet his welcoming committee.

"What kind of a meeting place is this?" he yelled. "Shotguns? For shit's sake guys, you sure as hell aren't IRS. Get me out of here!"

"Just get out of the car, Rogers! Stand up and step to the rear of the cruiser," said Davis. "We have to handcuff you to take you in for the interview and don't want any trouble, not one bit! Do you understand?"

In a low, stern voice, one of the armed men standing beside Davis amplified the instruction, "We know all about you, Jeep. I would be tickled pink if you resisted."

Jeep stiffened and locked his feet under the front seat of the cruiser, shouting that he wasn't going to be taken out and demanding to see the IRS agents who had called for his detention. All three of his adversaries responded, grabbing him by his hair and neck while pummeling his shins with shotgun butts. They dragged him onto the pavement cursing, his arms wildly flailing at them. His fight to stay upright and resist the handcuffs succeeded temporarily, but Patrolman Davis quickly administered a shot of pepper spray to his face and he collapsed onto the rear deck of the cruiser, choking and sobbing in excruciating pain. In seconds, he was cuffed, pulled upright, and his two escorts manhandled him inside the open doorway. One kept him physically subdued while the other slammed and secured the heavy prison door behind them.

Jeep was marched and half dragged across the dark courtyard, the blinding effects of the pepper spray preventing him from seeing anything of his darkened surroundings. He was lugged down several stairs, heard another door being opened and was thrust into an area of blinding, blurred light. A splash of cold water hit his face and a loud, gruff voice commanded him to stand where he was, not utter a sound and listen intently to his "briefing." With little pause, the voice continued.

"Welcome to your final destiny, Mr. Rogers, you sorry bastard! You are now the property of the people of the sovereign state of Montana. Our Supreme Court has reviewed every element of your murder trial from television and has declared that a great injustice to the laws and decency of mankind has been done in finding you innocent of your crimes in Illinois. This does not happen to be Illinois! Once news of your arrival came to us, our Supreme Court immediately began secret debate on your case and has now issued its summary judgment. You have been found guilty of murdering your wife and children and have therefore been sentenced to imprisonment right here in the Old Territorial Prison of Montana, for the rest of your goddamned miserable life. No appeals! And let me tell ya, you ain't about to ever escape from this place! Knock on stone Mr. Killer Rogers; you ain't gonna make a scratch on these walls.

"Now, we have a few rules here and you better listen carefully because they're not going to be repeated.

<u>One</u>, you are going to be locked up in solitary confinement all the time. You only get out of your cell to wash up and empty your slops each morning.

"<u>Two</u>, the three meals a day you get here are considered to be a privilege afforded only to those who behave. You mess up on anything and we cut off meals. Any bitchin' about the grub can get you the death penalty.

"<u>Three</u>, you are allowed no communication with the outside world, PERIOD!

"<u>Four</u>, you address all officers here as 'sir', and an attack or assault upon any one of us carries the death penalty which can be administered at our sole discretion.

"<u>Five</u>, silent hours are from lights out at 9:00 p.m. until 6:00 a.m. You may talk in moderate tones with other inmates during the daytime but no yelling or loud behavior will be tolerated.

"<u>Six</u>, reading is a privilege and you read anything we give out to you or nothing. No writing is allowed.

"You had the misfortune of joining us here during silent hours so I don't want to hear one goddamn whimper, gasp, fart or any sound out of you at all tonight! Officer, get him down to the shower crib, out of those pimp clothes and into some coveralls."

With that, still blinded by the pepper spray, Jeep was silently manhandled away from the lighted area and down a corridor. His lungs choked with anger and his face still broiled from the effects of the pepper spray. As much as he tried to conjure up a vision of his surroundings, Jeep's mind swirled in confusion, spinning away from gravity into clouds of fear and panic. His knees were weak and unstable as he was jerked to a halt near the rushing sound of shower water where he felt his handcuffs being removed.

"You will learn to manage just fine with cold water and brown laundry soap here, so get your fancy clothes off and move under that shower Mr. Prisoner, and do it right goddamn now! You have three minutes, so do a good job. You only get one of these a week."

He undressed and quickly began lathering under the cold spray with the large bar of soap thrust at him.

Blurs of dim light filtered into his vision as the water began diluting the burning pepper spray residue. Soon he was able to make out the faint dimensions of a concrete shower area and the form of a figure awaiting him. In what seemed like seconds, the shower was turned off, a towel thrown at him and he was ordered to get into a pair of orange nylon coveralls hanging on the nearest wall.

Hastily dressed in his new attire with hospital-type scuffs on his feet, he was taken in hand by the guard and led down a cold, dimly lit corridor with iron cell bars on each side. They paused mid-way and keys fumbled loudly into a locking mechanism. The cell door screeched open, and he was thrust into a void of nearly complete darkness.

As the door clanked shut behind him, Jeep struggled with his returning vision and he groped blindly into the black chasm to discern the kind of dungeon furnishings that might await him. His feet loudly collided with an empty bucket on the stone floor, and he lurched into an iron framework suspended from the wall by two heavy chains. The touch of a stuffed canvas mattress on its top revealed it to be a bunk, and he rolled forward onto it, deeply gasping for new breath to eradicate the painful burdens now crushing every cell of his body. He moaned, "Holy shit! I have been found guilty and sentenced to life imprisonment by the Montana Supreme Court?" Choking back sobs that painfully penetrated his throat, Jeep found his senses numbed with complete despair, confusion and shock that combined to transport him into an exhausted and troubled sleep.

In the dark of early morning, Jeep bolted upright, shuddering, his heart racing and his mind awash in spasms of panic. Someone came down the corridor banging as loud as possible on a dishpan, yelling, "Wake up time you sons a bitches! Get your lazy asses out of those sacks and get ready for wash up, slops and your morning gruel! MOVE IT!"

With scuffs still on his feet, he bounded to the floor and stood unsteadily facing the cell door. A dizzy, protective haze began to evaporate from his mind as the awareness of his situation returned to him. He had been in prison before, awaiting trial, but nothing could be as starkly unbelievable as the place he now found himself in. Was his situation as hopeless as he imagined? No one on earth had the slightest idea where he might be, and he painfully realized that to the outside world, he had completely vanished. In this new realm, he was fully aware that few, if any, cared.

As if in answer to his unspoken question, a subdued voice came from the cell to his right. "Hey! Are you really Jeep Rogers?"

He replied, "Hell yes I am. Who are you and what kind of goddamned place is this?"

The man answered, "You and I are at the end of our road, Jeep. This is the Old Territorial Prison of Montana. No one ever escaped from here and we are in the max area that was known as 'the dungeon', according to what the guard told me.

I remember reading all about your trial in Chicago. I think you belong here and they ought to let me out! Ha ha!"

"So who are you and what did you do to get in here? You know goddamned well that court didn't convict me, regardless of public opinion, and I am sure as hell going to court somewhere to get myself out of this stinking mess!" Jeep replied.

Muffled chuckles murmured around the corridor as another voice echoed out of the cell to Jeep's left. "Well I'll be goddamned! You sure you are Jeep Rogers the baseball guy huh? Holyshit!"

Again from the cell to the right, "I'm Eddie Weeks, originally from Superior, Montana. I got kidnapped a week ago, and I think I might be here for a good spell. Just got paroled in Washington after an eight year stretch for letting a couple of little girls molest me and was on leave going home to see my ailing mom. Sheriff nabbed me, and here I am. Boss guy says I got a life sentence to do for baby rape and murder, which I didn't commit. No sense me askin' why they snatched you up. What in hell you doin' in Montana anyhow?"

Before Jeep could reply, a guard passed down the corridor in front of his cell escorting another prisoner toward the wash room, carrying a slop bucket. Jeep spoke again, directing his attention to the cell on his left. "Yes, I'm the baseball guy and who are you? What are you in here for and how long?"

His last question brought a roll of laughter from at least four of the cells in the block. "How long? Haaaaa . . . haaaaa . . . . haaaaa!"

Then an answer came from the cell to his left. "Jeep, I'm Jimmy Mills and I have been here for six weeks, longest one of the bunch. Got bagged after doing little bits of bad time for different stuff up in the Havre area. You know, like several drug busts, armed robbery, accused of a couple of rapes but not convicted, assaults with guns and knives, whatever. So I guess someone got fed up with me being a bad boy and said I was a career criminal that shouldn't be runnin' around loose. Wound up right here and see no way out. Sentence? Hell man, we are all lifers in here; that's for damned sure!"

"That guy they just took to the stall is Bud Ferguson, a real bad ass! He did 8 years of a life sentence for murdering a girl filling station attendant when he was 17, then within a year wound up on trial for killing his dad and brother with a shotgun. He got off on that one with a slick lawyer and a self-defense plea. Next he did a murder rape of an old widow woman near Moise and was given life again. The old witness finally died in a rest home so Bud dug up a legal quirk and got set up for a new trial, which the state didn't feel it could win without their witness. Bud gets out on bond and suddenly winds up in here. Heh heh!"

Jeep became solemn as the dismal certainty of his situation became clear to him. He had innocently stumbled into a society that time had never changed from the old days of the Western frontier and he was now the victim of their brand of justice. No such thing could ever happen in a civilized place like Chicago or anywhere else, he thought. How could anyone imagine being captured and secretly prosecuted by a band of outlaws that the system knew nothing about? Or did they? That was a real highway patrolman that brought him here, and a legitimate constable in Big Fork kidnapped him. What was the name given to such gangsters in the Western movies? Vigilantes, that's it. Vigilantes. Goddamn, they held all the power!

CHAPTER 6

Only a Tourist Attraction

Janet Rivers found the rear museum entrance to the prison firmly locked when she attempted to follow the three men that had so quickly disappeared inside. Breathless after jogging the block-long wall to the front and main county jail entrance, she stumbled up the stairs and was immediately recognized by the night dispatcher and jailer. "Hey, Janet! What brings you in here at this time of night?"

"Well," she replied. "I just wanted to find out all about the celebrity criminal you just brought in here. What's happening with him, Mel?"

"What? Janet, what in hell are you talking about? A celebrity criminal like who?" He asked.

"Jeep Rogers, that's who! Look Mel, not five minutes ago, I saw a highway patrolman deliver him to the back gate and two of your guys with shotguns helped bring him inside. Geeze! Get that fake confused look off your face and level with me please!"

The jailer was sincerely astonished and barely able to utter his reply. "Miss Janet, we have no rear entrance to this jail, and that back area is under construction for the museum. I don't even have access to it. Jeep Rogers? Come on! I know there are county construction guys and night watchmen back there most of the time, old guys formerly law enforcement and so forth. Jeep Rogers? Naw, I'll bet you saw them bringing in one of their employees who had a little too many. You know, we kinda stick up for each other in the "fraternity", retired or not."

"Ok, Mel, that's plausible, so we will get it fixed right now. That crew back there has a telephone, right? So let's get out their number and give them a call and straighten this pipe dream out so that I can get back to sleep."

The jailer shuffled through some notes and open files, underlined an entry with his pencil and began dialing the desk telephone. He paused as the dial up sequence began, its tone barely overheard by Janet. After nearly a minute without answer, he gave Janet a quizzical look and reported, "Nobody there. They must be all gone home by now. Sorry."

"Well, there is always tomorrow. Please give me that number, Mel. I am positive I saw Jeep Rogers in their custody tonight and will check some more on it tomorrow.

Sure as hell I am not having illusions, but if so, I had better get busy on them as soon as possible! Ha! Thanks anyhow, and I hope you have a quiet shift. Good night!"

Janet had an early breakfast at the Biedler Motel after a broken, restless sleep in her van, and then drove out to the prison administration building where she joined several dozens of law enforcement personnel gathered in the "war room" for a briefing. She quickly armed herself with part of the endless supply of coffee, exchanged greetings with friends from the locality and surrounding counties, and made her way around the room to intercept Captain Harold Miller, district commander of the Montana Highway Patrol.

"Hi Harold," she said. "I hope we don't have to meet under these circumstances often. It seems like you never get over to Helena with enough time to spare for coffee or lunch."

"Hello again, Janet." He replied. "I sure would like to see you there and have always had good intentions, but it seems like every damned time some kind of emergency comes up and I have to leave. So what's new in the print business?"

"Well, Harold, a prison break like this is news if it doesn't happen too often!" she chuckled. "So who was the guy from your department making a stop at the old prison about 10 o'clock last night?"

Miller answered with a curious look, "A stop at the old prison? No one that I know of. All of my local officers were in here to assist on the search, and I can't think of anyone in town or offline who would be there. We had to deal with more remote road junctions and suspect locations than we had coverage for. Everyone was tied up on overtime."

"Harold, I was parked across the street from the museum back entrance last night, trying to get a little shuteye, when a ruckus woke me up. Right across the street from my van, there was a patrol car and an officer who delivered some guy to two others waiting with shotguns.

They cuffed him, manhandled him inside the back gate and the patrolman immediately departed. It seemed pretty strange that they would be using the back entrance to the museum when the front jail was open and Mel sitting in there doing nothing. I talked with him briefly, and he seemed to know nothing about the whole deal. What do you make of that, Harold?"

Captain Miller paused before answering. In deep concentration, he slowly rubbed his chin stubble with his right hand. A little gold and sapphire ring on his pinky finger glistened in the flood of the room's fluorescent lighting. "I sure can't explain anything about what you saw, Janet, but will surely look into it and give you the complete low-down. Was there anything else unusual about that encounter last night? What did Mel have to say about it?"

"This will get you, Harold." she replied, "I could swear that guy in custody was that goddamned killer, Jeep Rogers! I told Mel about it and he probably thinks I'm nuts! Anyhow, he felt that the incident was simply a patrolman bringing in one of the "inner" law enforcement guys to sleep one off. That's a possibility, even though I know the guy was a dead ringer for Rogers. Hell, Captain, there aren't enough black guys around these parts to count on both hands and surely no duplicates for the notorious Jeep Rogers!"

"I would never question your powers of observation and detail, Janet," he replied. "There has to be a good explanation for this somehow, but I truly doubt that anyone brought a drunken Jeep Rogers into the museum area to sleep off a binge. I promise to get back to you on it, but right now I have to tune in to the scheme of things here so that I can deploy my troops. I will be in touch and thanks for bringing this to me."

With that courteous closure to the conversation, Miller made his way to the map area where the extended ring of search responsibilities was being assigned. It always amazed Janet at how such detail could be gathered in such a short time and dispatched in almost random fashion. However, the terrain around Scribner was known with much more certainty to the lawmen than to any escapee and she was sure the three would be recaptured by nightfall. As much as she tried to focus on tactics and the displayed search pattern, the impact of the prior night's incident gnawed at her mind.

She mingled with the group for a few minutes then quietly took leave of them to find a phone and call the museum. She was unaware that Captain Miller had also departed.

Janet was relieved to connect with the retired sheriff Tom Kelly, and she asked him if he had an explanation for bringing in the criminal celebrity, Jeep Rogers the night before. "Just what in hell are you talking about, little lady? That Rogers guy is playing the jet set high road far away from these parts for sure. No way he would show up around here."

"Now look, Tom, I know I saw him being offloaded from a trooper car behind your courtyard last night and hustled in here. All I want to know is what is happening.

We've been friends for a good many years and you know you can trust me. What's the deal, huh?"

"Janet," he replied, "We have no way of handling any prisoners in the museum area here, which ain't even half finished, and anything like that would be workin' out front where the regular jail is. You really have me confused with a pipe dream like that one, although I don't doubt your way with the truth one bit. You are mighty welcome to stop by and have a look around anytime it suits you, ya hear?"

She cordially closed out the conversation and was somewhat relieved by the offer to inspect things, but her intuition still gave her unambiguous sensations that she was being stonewalled all around. Janet had one more call to make before she got back into the story surrounding the prison escape. Charles might have picked up a fragment of information from one of the locals about this surprising Jeep Rogers development.

"Hello, Charles. Sorry to interrupt your busy schedule, but while I have been out here in Scribner following the manhunt thing, something really strange came up. I wonder if you might know anything of it."

"Hmmm . . . What kind of mystery have you stumbled into now, Janet?"

"Well, I was catching some shuteye last night in my van, which was parked on the street behind the old prison. Sometime near 2:00 A.M. this patrol cruiser came up and a ruckus ensued that woke me up.

"I stirred around to see the patrolman and a couple of guys with shotguns man-handling a man into the back gate. So help me, the prisoner was Jeep Rogers! I have been asking questions about it all day and no one knows a thing about it! Have you heard anything of the kind about the capture of Jeep Rogers?"

"Wow! Janet, I have no idea how such a thing could happen up here. Nope, not one word about anything like that going on, especially with that miserable super star murdering bastard! Surely the Bureau would have some kind of local contact around to tell us about it. Nothing at all involving us."

"Yep," Charles replied, "no mistake about us keeping up a few ideas on where he might be from time to time, and I will let you know as sure as I find out something.

Meanwhile, be careful out there and hold tight on this matter until you and I can discuss it at more length. Ok?"

"You are the light of my life, Charles! I can't wait to get back to Helena so that we can discuss all kinds of things!" She smiled to herself, hearing his murmured reply as she hung up.

As she left the public telephone area, she almost stumbled into Captain Miller as he was rushing back to the briefing room. "Oops," he said. "We just got a break, did you hear?"

"Nope, what's up Captain?"

"We got word over the radio a few minutes ago that a posse party with dogs crossed the trail of the escapees and now has them in custody up by Georgetown Lake. We will wrap up the details as soon as they get them back here."

"Good work, Captain, all the way around! I have to head back on over to Helena anyhow, but be sure to give me the names of the guys who did the work so that I can give them special attention in my story. I will be in touch."

CHAPTER 7

Mystery Wrapped Inside an Enigma

On her way back to Helena, Janet was unaware of passing through the little railroad villages of Avon and Elliston, her thoughts completely absorbed in the Jeep Rogers enigma. She had no realization of space or time until she crested Lookout Pass and began mentally setting priorities for her investigation, based first on whatever kind of information Charles had for her. She would get to the bottom of this mess somehow and it would be a story of real magnitude if her suspicions were valid. As she passed eastward across Helena's main street, Last Chance Gulch, she felt a rush of excitement about the possibilities of the mystery she had fallen into. On her way to Jorgensen's for a light dinner, she made a cell-phone call to Charles. She recorded the time and left a message for him to meet her there, reminding him that the dinner and cocktails would be on her.

As she angled southward to the capitol complex, and then again eastward, she began mentally sorting out the questions she needed answered, especially the one dealing with what kind of power base might be able to pull off such a maneuver with a "not guilty criminal" the likes of Rogers. Obviously there was some kind of illegitimate activity involving members of legitimate law enforcement. If Jeep Rogers really had been kidnapped, this was a crime loaded with high felony charges and monumental public interest. Very bright and determined people had to be in on this one.

The plot required the gathering of lots of information about Rogers, his whereabouts, plans, means of transport, arrival times, coordination of his kidnap, transportation and place of confinement. For how long? Is this an isolated incident? How many people would it take to accomplish this kind of mission? Why the old prison? What were they going to do with him other than haul him around . . . as a trophy . . . what? Is something worse in store for him? How could they keep others from knowing about this caper? "Wow! Enough stuff to give me a really big headache!" muttered Janet aloud as she rolled into Jorgensen's parking lot.

Janet was nursing her second margarita when Charles arrived. He was anxious and perplexed about what she had witnessed in Scribner. As he ordered his usual double martini, he explained that the Bureau had only been able to establish that Rogers was missing and had made a flight plan from Salt Lake City to Jackson Hole, Wyoming, four days ago. They had not yet confirmed whether or not he was there. "Close enough to these parts that something of the kind you suspect might be possible." he noted. "So what is the whole of what you think is going on here, huh?"

They paused to order their meals and a refill on their drinks, while Janet assembled her thoughts around the new information Charles had provided. She pondered deeply on the fact that Rogers could very easily be in the locality, and he was as secretive as he could be about any of his goings and comings. It was very logical that he could have slipped into some remote part of Montana and surely there was lots of that available!

"Ok, my lovin' Charlie. I am assuming that Rogers is here, and that some avenging hero types have taken it upon themselves to mete out the kind of justice that everyone expected of the system, except for a corrupt, racist Chicago jury. Further, let's assume that these elite, avenging Montanans are also members of our law enforcement. What would those brief, introductory thoughts mean to you, Charles?"

"Well, Janet, that conjures up one helluva mess for Montana law enforcement, for sure! Seems to me that it would possibly involve very few players, but ones who are sure as hell "right wing" about almost anything. They would be known to others as ones who would take the law into their own hands and be proud of it."

Dinner arrived as Janet began with the details of her suspicions. "Charlie, wouldn't their antics . . . er behavior be known to others? Especially to their bosses or other links in the system?"

"Well, it would be hard to conceal that kind of character, even up here in good old Montana, but I still think it need not involve many people to carry out the kidnapping of a guy like Rogers."

"What if he is not the only one, lover?"

"Ooooh . . . do you mean you have evidence of others? Wow! That could change the nature of things a lot."

"Nope, no evidence or a clue. Only surmising out loud, dear Charlie. But just suppose such a thing was going on and involved multiples of bad guys. What would you think then and how would Montana be able to deal with it? What would it take to fix it?"

"Hmmm . . . seems to me that they would have to be murdering the victims and hiding their remains where they could never be found. That is such a serious mess that it would have to involve not only law enforcement but part of the judiciary, I suppose. Be kind of like the old vigilante days where the real law enforcement had to be carried out in secrecy and it was a complete 'system' of justice unto itself. That is why the first such vigilante orders of law in the early days of the West were instituted by the Masonic Lodge.

"The Free Masons had the only secret order in which one member could trust another and their rites had long been practiced in utmost secrecy. They, therefore, could hold 'grand jury' proceedings, trials and sentencing in complete obscurity, and carry their work out with fellow Masons charged with enforcement. One such fellow was the famous J. X. Biedler who was one of the original vigilantes. He was known to be the fastest and most accurate gun-slinger in Montana Territory. That motel you stayed in was named after him. Some of the things they did may not have been legal by modern standards, but it was all that was available then, and their involvement gave us the first law and order in the territory. Those old timers are true heroes to lots of us native Montana folk. Seems reasonable that some of the law up here would feel that way too."

As they finished their meal with coffee and fresh apple pie, Charlie continued, "So you see, Janet, just supposing that is what the motive might be . . . having an involvement of the proportion you imagine . . . overturning it could be a really big deal. Check out our Montana history of the early era vigilantes, the ones who secretly tried, condemned and hanged the robber sheriff Henry Plummer and his gang. Tell me if you come across a single vigilante who was accused or even rumored to be a criminal and was ultimately brought to justice for it. Nope. You will find none. They are all illuminated in our books as pillars of our ancestry and true heroes who tamed the rugged, lawless West.

"To bring it all up to date, let's follow your angle about a large conspiracy. It would first depend upon absolute secrecy and ironclad trust of the kind that preserved the brotherhood of Free Masons for what, several thousands of years? Secondly, it would require the strictest and most capable kind of management. Last, it would have to involve every level of law enforcement from the beat cop up through supervision, perhaps prosecutors and judges."

Intently absorbing every word, Janet sipped her coffee as Charles continued.

"Together, in this day and age, the whole matrix that would be required would be impossible to put together. In short, providing you really did see Jeep Rogers, it would have to be a very isolated case exercised by a bare minimum of three or four individuals. That's what I think."

"Well, Charlie, that is a very thorough and scholarly viewpoint on just about everything I was beginning to imagine. But let's just pretend that I really did see Rogers and that he is now being held a prisoner in some part of the old prison that has been designated as the territorial museum. If that should be fact, what would one do to expose the kidnapping and what might be the risks?"

"I think you should low-key it until you get some other confirmation supporting your sighting of who you think was Rogers. If you do, bring me into it so that I can help out with some kind of strategy and resources to break the thing open. You should steer clear of visibility because some people would have a lot to lose and probably wouldn't go down without a serious fight. Surely a lot of very earnest threats would come down upon anyone who might know of or divulge their little program, and I sure wouldn't want that to be you."

"Ok, Charlie. Enough for now, and we don't want the rest of our night to be disrupted by such a slight issue, now would we? Let's get out of here and back to our little nest where we can talk of other things like . . . carpet tacks and sealing wax, and cabbages and kings!" She winked and grinned as she donned her jacket and made her way with the dinner tab to the cashier.

CHAPTER 8

Birthplace of the Vigilantes

Some 80 miles or so southwest of Helena lies the remote little cattlemen's town of Dillon, Montana. With a population of some 2,000 souls, it is a place whose character, size and economy have remained about the same since its founding 150 years ago. Dillon's streets were trod by the likes of Henry Plummer, vigilante marshal J. X. Biedler, Lame Deer Sheriff Jeremia (Liver Eatin') Johnson, robber Clubfoot George Ives and his gang, first governor Sidney Edgerton, Lilly Langtree, Generals Miles and Custer, Jim Bridger, Buffalo Bill Cody and Hallelujah Ezekiel Jones . . . the first real Christian minister, occult Ouija medium, medicine salesman, and faith healer to come into the early mining camps of Montana Territory.

In the early days, Dillon was also a kind of communications junction between Butte, Virginia City, and Bannack, Montana. Nearby, is the old Spook Davis ranch, still identified as such but worked today by great grandson Herb Davis, rancher and retired sheriff of Beaverhead County. In the rear of the ranch lies a small sliver of acreage adjoining B.L.M. land. Still standing on this tract is the old livery and way station that once fronted the postal road between Butte and Virginia City and a few of its out-buildings. It was named then and remains known today as Spook Davis' Grub and Tail Roost. A fragment of the early day postal road is the only access to Spook's, but its use is governed by a "No Trespassing" sign and a chained, locked gate. All are visible and within shooting distance of the Davis' front porch.

If one should happen to pass by the Davis place on a night when signs of a late presence were apparent, one could see in the distance, kerosene lamps lighting the windows of Spook's way station, shadows moving about inside, and a wisp of smoke drifting upward from the iron stove's chimney.

The place had been kept in working condition using the original furnishings and items of bare necessity that includes the iron cook stove, white porcelain dishes, a granite coffee pot and kettle, tin cups, brass cuspidors, iron fry pans and broiler, oil lamps, and one long wooden dining table. Well-worn pegs line the inside walls. Several antique but perfectly working Winchester rifles stand in a few corners around the main cabin, and small stacks of rifle and pistol ammunition sit on various window sills. The mountain cabin motif is enhanced by the tanned pelts of mountain lions, badgers and a buffalo robe hung as artwork. Ten wooden chairs sit randomly on the rough-sawed, creaky plank floor.

An open cabinet near the stove filled with canned fruits, vegetables, condensed milk, Salt, pepper, sugar, tobacco, coffee, stick matches, several bottles of Canadian and expensive Scotch whiskey is a give-away to present day use. Bar glasses, cigarette papers and an assortment of well-used pipes confirm a predominately male décor. But the most important piece of original artwork hangs inside, above the front entrance. It is a crude wooden sign painted with whitewash and inscribed by jack knife that reads, "VIGILANCE 3-7-77".

In modern times, Spook's place played perhaps its most important function ever as the conference center and retreat for the Justice Brigade's Council of Ten. It was there on the night after Janet Rivers' dinner conference with Charles Gettys that a late night driver on the county road by the Davis place might have seen lights from the windows of the old way station off in the distance. It could appear that possibly a range rider was making use of the outpost for the night but very few others knew for sure that whenever the lamps were lit in Spook's cabin, things of much higher importance were going on. The Council of Ten was now gathered there in emergency session.

Shadowy figures of men, dimly revealed by the glow of oil lamps, moved around inside the room. Faces were indistinct but here and there, the glint of a badge, large belt buckle or burnished handle of a sidearm caught the yellow light. Floorboards creaked under foot, crackling sounds came from the fire inside the iron stove, accompanied by the occasional scraping of a large coffee pot as cups were refilled. The room quieted when a deep, hollow voice announced, "Greetings brothers! We are here tonight to deal with an exposure of great importance to our organization and come up with a plan to fix it." He went on to describe the discoveries Janet Rivers had made and where she was going with them.

Another voice spoke from the shadows, "Guys she is going to dig into this thing and even though we know that what she saw is real, there is no way in hell we can prove different to her. She simply ain't gonna go for any other flimsy story that we might conjure up, and we agree that she will never bite on any suggestion that she was dreaming up this stuff. Hell, we all respect her as much as we do each other. She's the best advocate that law and order ever had in this country so maybe we should consider getting her into the J.B. and that would make sure we are all protected."

"Well, John, that's about the best idea I've heard yet on how to fix up this mess, but I know for sure that she is honest to the core, naïve about a lot of imperfections in this here life and probably wouldn't flinch once before spilling out what a bunch of bloody outlaws we are. Hell, we couldn't fault her for that anyhow because if you respected our purposes, the methods would make sense just like in the old days. But I don't think she is of a mind to do either and that is why I would vote against bringing her into the Brigade."

Another spoke, "Shit, gentlemen, I guess we will just hafta try to lie and bluff her out of her curiosities, alienate her from information and hope she doesn't run across any other trip wires to the truth. Geeze! I sure as hell don't like running a game like this on such a fine, loyal citizen as she is. We need some more ideas here."

The deep voice of their leader interrupted, "Well, brothers, I think we all agree that if this was anyone other than Janet Rivers, our job would be much simpler. She might just disappear. However, I think we can keep her isolated on this one case and let it play on out, excepting that it won't reveal Jeep Rogers. She can't be absolute sure it was him and we have to work out a plan for someone else to take a minor fall for what is going on in the prison. Charles, I think you would have the biggest responsibility for controlling her and carrying out most of it. You are going to need a lot of help and I will get to work on that. For sure, we will not be using the old prison as a holding area anymore."

The leader of the group called for a vote and it passed without objection. A plan was concocted to cover all potential areas of further exposure and items of diversion were delegated. The meeting concluded by early sunrise on Saturday morning and the members departed singly, ten minutes apart. The last one out closed and locked the gate.

Spook Davis' Grub and Tail Roost

That same morning, Janet arose early and alone, as was customary to being the companion of an FBI agent. His late night call out was one of the discreet things that they took in stride and she never inquired about any such occasion. With her morning coffee, she skimmed through the *Helena Standard,* editing and mentally critiquing her coverage of the prison break and apprehension. She chuckled over the accolades she had generously included for the three deputies who were the point men for the re-capture of the bad guys. They would be mortified with embarrassment by now.

Freshly into her second cup of coffee, Janet began rewriting, scrutinizing and assembling her notes on the gnawing matter of Jeep Rogers. She was trying to ferret out something she subconsciously knew was in there but couldn't fix for certain. Janet spent several hours at the kitchen table with her laptop, charting, re-arranging, expanding and analyzing her information before the target of her efforts flashed into her mind.

It was something Charles had said about the numbers of kidnappings that would require an impossibly large body of law enforcement. He had suggested that such an operation would require the involvement of all levels of the judicial system and probably involve murder or "execution". All such motives would be quite far beyond the limits of reality. She felt that Charles was hung up on the colorful days of the vigilantes which he firmly believed could never come again to protect a civilized society. Janet had all kinds of doubts about his philosophy and felt sure that there were some frustrated police types around who would actively pursue such means to "save us all from the pain and decay of justice turned against us."

Why would such involvement be so impossible? What would prevent a small number of police hard-liners or vigilantes from arranging such a thing and randomly conspiring to make the bad guys disappear? Why would the judiciary need to be involved if they didn't know about such goings-on?

"Where is the first strand to get me started unraveling this ball of yarn?" She muttered aloud. "I know! It's Tom Kelly's invitation to look the place over any time I want to! I think I will take him up on that today."

At that point the phone rang. It was Charles calling to report that he was involved in helping out with compiling the final trial evidence on an Indian reservation murder case. He said he would be home early in the day and asked if she had plans for anything. She told him of Davis' invitation and said she had planned to look the place over. Charles commented that he thought that was a good idea and warmly closed the conversation. Minutes later, Janet arrived at the front entrance of the old prison and her knock on the door was answered by a smiling Tom Kelly. "Hello and welcome again to our humble digs here. Have you decided to take a tour of the place?"

"Yes", she replied. "I want to learn how this place was originally laid out and see what kind of partitions you have arranged to make it into a museum and offices for the sheriff."

While unrolling some large charts onto an office table, Kelly began, "I guess we can begin with going over a composite of the prison layout as it was originally built, including early day additions and alterations. Right here, you can see the dimensions of each floor, beginning with the lower level which was once called the 'dungeon'. That was where the most serious offenders were kept or those who went into solitary confinement when they couldn't behave or adjust to normal prison life. The red dimension lines on the plans show the areas which we have reworked to split out the sheriff's office and county jail in front from this rear area where we are constructing the museum. I can bring these along if you care to look around."

"Sure," Janet replied. "I am most interested in how you are going to handle tours in here, and most of all what kind of conditions the prisoners lived with in the lower, solitary cells."

"You picked the most interesting of the hard life places in here, Janet. But as you can see over there, the entrance to that area is off limits because it's a hazard getting up and down the decaying stairs. All of that will be restored to just the way it was but is now only a moldy, dank piece of the underground facility that we haven't had budget money to fix up. We can take a walk around through the upper, main cellblock levels if you want. Plenty to talk about there, and you can find numerous bullet holes and marks left behind from the riots of 1954 and 1957, which were subdued by the Montana National Guard."

"I'm sure that is all very interesting, Tom, but I was primarily interested in that basement area with the solitary cells. Are you sure it isn't safe to take a quick peek down there?"

"I'm very sure of that, Janet. It's a hard-hat area at best, and I don't feel safe prowling around in there myself. Sorry but that will have to wait until a later tour. I know you think we may have some kind of mysterious, hidden detention area in here but that is really an impossibility. Sometimes I have wished we did have such a thing though."

"What do you mean by that, Tom?"

"Law and order is becoming as liberal here as it has around the country and it seems like everyone is hell bent to setting the guilty loose. It seems to me that we should have some means of restoring a sense of public confidence in the system of justice that we once had in these parts and not make it so easy for the worst offenders."

"Are you talking about the vigilantes?"

"You know, Janet, the state patrol still wears their secret code, '3-7-77', on their shoulder patches. Must be some kind of nostalgic symbol or something, huh? But it does make one think about the old days and those earnest citizens of the Freemason Lodge who took it upon themselves to bring the rule of law to this dangerous and forlorn part of the country. I was only thinking how regrettable it is that such an effort would be so impossible nowadays."

"Sure is, Tom, regrettable. Well, since I can't get to see the old dungeon area right now, I guess I will only have to imagine what crude conditions the prisoners endured there. I will save that visit when I can look the whole thing over and may write a good story about it. Thanks again, I'll be seeing you later on and appreciate your taking the time with me today."

"On the house, Janet. Looking forward to your next visit. Here, let me show you out."

Janet departed, barely able to conceal her consternation with the fruitless result of her visit. She was convinced more than ever that she had found the source of her suspicions and that was the secret lockup in the old prison basement. She would now have to force the issue somehow and she would need Charles' fullest cooperation in order to do it. On her way back to Helena, she mentally rehearsed the only strategy that could work and that was to have Charles secure a federal warrant from Judge R.J. Smith of the 72nd Judicial District in Butte, to search the old territorial prison.

Her mind searched through questions and tactics. On what legal basis could she make the petition work? What charges would elicit federal intervention over state jurisdiction? Charles would have to initiate it all with a strong affidavit. Would her suspicions be convincing enough for probable cause to issue the warrant?

First of all, she will allege official corruption and conspiracy on the part of state and local police as the root of the entire scheme. That would require federal intervention for sure. Beyond that, the principal crime would be wrongful imprisonment and anything associated with it. The number of counts to the crimes would depend on how many unfortunate victims were found as a result of the search. Of course, if nothing came of the search, virtually no harm done. Everyone could say "oops . . . sorry", and go back to their normal routines. Tonight, she would take the issue up with Charles and work on it until he gave in.

The night passed into early dawn before their debate was resolved in Janet's favor. Charles summoned the energy to type up an affidavit and called the judge's office for an appointment. They would meet with him at 1:00 P.M. on the following day in Butte, Montana. After taking a quick shower and shaving, Charles began packing a light bag for an unplanned trip to Harlem, Montana, near the Crow Indian Reservation. As he poured another cup of coffee on his way out, Charles hurriedly explained to Janet that he had to help a fellow agent interview a witness to a crime committed on the reservation. He would be back in time to pick her up and meet with Judge Smith.

"By the way, here's something for you to think seriously about tonight while I'm gone. I am reconsidering taking that S.A.C. job in Olympia and thinking about making an honest thing out of this relationship so that we can move there together. Don't answer right now, sleep on it. Bye!"

"Wow! What a way he has of closing a conversation," she mumbled through an excited chuckle.

CHAPTER 9

The Council of Ten

The oil lamps again burned late at night at the Davis place while the Justice Brigade held another session to discuss tactics to deal with the new developments brought about by Janet Rivers. After the debate had ranged through innumerable options, the leader summarized the situation and gave his recommendations.

"Brothers, as it stands right now, I think we have a good loop around this whole mess and it is going to play out with a happy ending for us all."

"John," said another, "I think I see what he is suggesting here. If we get those prisoners out of there, then there is only the evidence of an unknown 'john doe' or someone being held there and now gone off to parts unknown. No one would have to admit that they knew the identities of the prisoners. Let's just say it was a temporary means used to scare the hell out of town drunks, bullies, undesirable vagrants or scum like that."

From a dark corner of the cabin entered another faceless voice. "Sure, but that would still place criminal responsibility on the ones they charge. Supposing they plead guilty and admit to unlawfully holding or detaining certain individuals on an irregular basis and then letting them go after a few days. The investigation would branch out into maybe a town cop who brought them there and whoever might be involved in supplying the groceries or toiletries while they were incarcerated. May not be such a big deal after all."

A fourth party interjected, "Well, on a plea of guilty, I think we could deal with that quite quickly and limit the harm done to any one of the accused."

Again, the leader, "Ok then brothers, does anyone have more to add before I summarize things here?" After a brief uninterrupted pause, he began, "First of all, let's get the prisoners out tonight . . . er, this morning, into vehicles inside the courtyard. Since we can't take the risk of being discovered moving all five to one place, we'll split them up. Get Jimmy Mills and Bud Ferguson up to Snowshoe and drop them into the well. Carry another one to the old brewery building in Virginia City and two to the old stone powder magazine in Phillipsburg. Let's get their necks stretched and be done with them.

Secondly, we allow the warrant to proceed and alert the players that are going to be bagged to prepare to plead guilty and confess to the charges we have discussed here. We will let due process take its course from there and, God willing, justice will prevail from there on out. Questions? Meeting adjourned!"

June 18, Phillipsburg, Montana.

"Well, let's see here. You be the notorious, murdering Jeep Rogers and you other guy must be that dirty, rotten little bastard, Edward Weeks. Right? Welcome to Phillipsburg, Montana, gents." The man speaking lovingly ran his hand down a dirty, cold stone and concrete wall. "This here's the magazine for blasting powder from the early mining days. It's walls are two feet thick to protect the powder from thievery. It's set off a ways from the town so that if she ever touched off and blew, no townsfolk would come to harm. Therefore, gents, you can scream and holler and raise hell all you want but no one's gonna hear you, so you might just as well behave.

"I'm Elmer Brown, retired lawman and caretaker here. That man there's my brother, Ed Brown. You're gonna be in our custody until someone else decides what to do with you. We might be along in years but that won't mean you should think about trying to tackle either of us. We'll feed you and care for you for as long as needed, so there's no reason for you getting shot here, even though either one of us would just as soon gut shoot you as look at you. So don't try any monkey business and we'll all get along just fine."

Rogers spoke up. "Mr. Lawman, why not just shoot us and forget about keeping us at all?"

"Well, sonny boy, first of all, you ain't been sentenced to death yet. You have been sentenced by an honorable judicial committee of fine citizens to spend the rest or your miserable lives rotting in a dark little jail cell. Secondly, unlawful killing is frowned on in Montana but that doesn't include self defense, being shot whilst interfering with a lawman doing his duty or trying to escape from custody. Does that straighten it all out for you?"

Sunlight glinted on the gold ring with the dark blue stone displayed on Brown's right little finger as he patted his hip pistol for emphasis. Jeep Rogers had seen the same ring worn by others, several times before, and noted the same on the hand of the brother, Ed.

CHAPTER 10

Search Warrant

Janet was ecstatic over the cheerful news Charles had left with her the previous day relative to their future together, but when they met in Butte at about 11:00 A.M. he was too engrossed in preparing for the judge to discuss any of it. He was focused on the affidavit and the argument in favor of proceeding with the search. Surely Janet would have a major role in convincing the judge with as much credibility and enthusiasm as she had won her argument with him.

Their meeting with the judge began promptly at one o'clock.

"Your honor, probable cause to issue a warrant is based on this witness' unwavering testimony about the presence of Jeep Rogers at the Old Territorial Prison late at night or in the early morning hours of June 14 of this year, and her allegation that he was in the custody of armed persons acting as captors. The matter is brought to your jurisdiction because she alleges that the transportation used to bring Rogers to the prison was a uniformed cruiser bearing the markings of Montana Highway Patrol. As such, she is asking federal intervention on a suspected conspiracy governed by U.S. codes under the Official Corruption Act. She further alleges that a uniformed officer driving that car assisted in turning Mr. Rogers over to two armed men who were present at the back entrance to the prison. These allegations also point to official corruption on the part of the Montana law enforcement authorities which allows for federal investigation and criminal prosecution. When she inquired of the jailer about the incident, he said she was mistaken about what she claimed to have witnessed."

"Ms. Rivers, I know both of you quite well and have no doubts that your allegations should be taken very seriously. Do you have anything else to add beyond your sworn statement to those items briefed here by Mr. Gettys?"

"Well, your honor, I feel that the activity that I suspect is going on at the old prison could not be carried out without a great number of people secretly conspiring and participating in it. I believe it is on the order and magnitude of a statewide vigilante committee but has no means of substantiating that theory. Your granting of a warrant to search the prison should yield evidence that could bring all of that to light."

"Alright. I hereby grant the order to search the specified premises and seize any and all evidence that may be there which may bring light upon the kind of criminal activity alleged, as befits the interests and jurisdiction of federal law and this court.

"Mr. Gettys, I want this warrant served no later than 10:00 P.M. tomorrow night and I presume you will muster the resources from both the F.B.I. and Federal Marshall's office in order to do so."

"Thank you, your honor. I will contact a fellow agent from Butte and get U.S. Marshall Scott from Great Falls to assist. I don't think we will have any problems getting it all done by tomorrow evening."

"Thank you both for being here. You had better hope that your concerns bear some reasonability on this. I am going way out on a limb here with lots of personal trust in your judgment. Don't let me down."

On the way back from the federal courthouse, Janet's thoughts were rampant over Charles' latest change in plans about marriage and the move to Olympia, Washington. However, she forced herself to contain the discussion to the elements of solving her mystery at the prison and getting in on the service of the warrant. Charles put his foot down on the latter.

As he pulled to the curb in front of her apartment, he explained, "Janet, I know the privilege of the press and all of that but I really cannot consent to your being there for the search. It could turn out to be a sensitive one and could expose you to a lot of danger. What if the group is as large as you suspect and we get only a couple of them? You are the key witness to this thing and surely would be the likely target of any retaliation. You sit tight, be watchful and cautious, and let me keep you posted by phone on the developments. I plan on executing the warrant by 9:00 in the morning so I have to get scampering to get the others here and brief them.

"Oh, by the way, and I know this is a key issue too. That was a proposal of marriage I gave you yesterday and it did include a move for us both to a new area away from here. No need to answer now but I hope you have a couple of positive things to say about it."

"Oof! You sure don't waste time with boring formalities, do you? Well, since you qualified your brief quip as an actual proposal, I accept! And I shall be happy to be your wife and homemaker in beautiful Olympia, Washington. So there! Brief answer right back atcha!"

Charles responded with a big hug and long kiss. "That would make me the happiest agent in the service and the proudest! Details and plans to follow. Right now . . . back to work."

The next day the warrant was served on Tom Kelly, the only person of standing at the old prison. A thorough inspection of the entire premises produced no inmates or anyone else of responsibility for the occupation and reconstruction of the prison. However, a great deal of evidence was gathered in the basement area. The solitary confinement cells revealed telling indications of recent occupancy by one or more individuals. When confronted with this evidence, Tom confessed that he and others working with him had, from time to time, jailed drifters and suspected junkies to give them a good scare and firm notice to leave these parts for good. It was done more or less as a prank, but they realized that such things were unlawful. They tried to justify their behavior by implying that they were performing a reasonable service to the community that in reality didn't permanently harm anyone. Kelly implicated Ruben Tyler, local grocery store proprietor, as the one who supplied food and toiletries for the prisoners, and Frank Meador, Scribner constable, as the one who made the "arrests".

Tyler and Meador were arrested within an hour of the completion of the search and all three gave sworn confessions to their respective roles in the unlawful imprisonment over the past year of as many as seven persons officially unknown to them. They adamantly denied having brought anyone into the prison with the name of Jeep Rogers.

The suspects were taken to the Butte jail where federal prisoners were detained while awaiting court process. They jointly employed the services of semi-retired Butte defense attorney William J. Fromberg and their arraignment was scheduled for June 22, before U.S. Justice Smith. Janet Rivers was there to witness the proceedings, along with members of all of the major press services of Montana. At their arraignment, all pleaded guilty to charges of wrongful imprisonment, conspiracy and aiding and abetting the commission of felonies. A sentencing hearing was scheduled for June 28, and then all were freed on their own recognizance and returned to Scribner where they were feted in an impromptu reception attended by over 100 citizens of the community.

As they left the courthouse, Janet could no longer hide her frustration over the investigation and arrests. "Charles, this is a complete sham! I know there was at least one highway patrolman involved in this mess and it should be obvious to anyone that somehow, information about the search was leaked and they removed the prisoners, probably the night before. I am dead certain that I saw Jeep Rogers in their custody and nothing can change my mind about that. There is one helluva big, stinking kangaroo court thing going on here and I will get to the bottom of it!"

"Janet, we took that place apart over at least 12 hours and never came up with any evidence that would indicate that other than a few 'john doe' prisoners could have been kept there. We have all kinds of fingerprints but none linking us to any known person, including Jeep Rogers. We went after that specifically. We have only the stories of the defendants as to what went on there and nothing to contradict them. What else can we do? Unless you can think of something else I can pursue, you are spinning your wheels on this one."

"Maybe so, Charles, but somewhere, sometime new news about this thing will seep to the surface and you will know I am right. But, for the present, I am willing to let it take a back seat to my real priority and that is to become Mrs. Gettys."

"Well, we are going to have a lot of work compressed into a short period of time. I have already emailed the area supervisor of my intention to accept the job out there, and I have to take four days away to interview. That's only a formality but will also give me a chance to be briefed and meet the players. The big glitch is that I have to be in place by mid-July and that allows nothing much for a formal wedding, honeymoon, house-hunting, moving of our goods. Not much time for anything!"

"Charles, I don't mind a small wedding with just a few close friends and neither of us has family close enough to attend. Maybe I could take the interview trip with you and look around some. Then we can get back here and have the movers merge our stuff, ship it all and have it stored until we are ready to call for it. But how about us getting married first?

Their plans unfolded along the lines Janet suggested and they were married by a justice of the peace two days later in the company of a couple of dozen friends. After working around one urgent obligation after another, they found a rushed window of opportunity to attend the sentencing hearing on June 28.

Judge Smith was just beginning as they came into the courtroom, "The court will now hear responses to the charges against defendants Thomas Lincoln Kelly, Ruben

James Tyler and Franklin Scott Meador, to which each has entered a plea of guilty. Are you counsel for these three defendants, Mr. Fromberg?"

"Yes, I am, your honor."

"Very well. Mr. Kelly, you are charged with seven felony counts of unlawful imprisonment and corresponding counts of conspiracy to commit these crimes. You have entered a plea of guilty to those charges. Do you wish to change your plea?"

"Nope, your honor, I have confessed and plead guilty."

Mr. Franklin Scott Meador, you are charged with seven felony counts of wrongful imprisonment and conspiracy to commit these crimes. You have previously entered a plea of guilty to the same. Do you wish to change your plea?"

"I plead guilty, your honor."

Mr. Ruben James Tyler, you are charged with willfully aiding and abetting the commission of felony federal crimes, i.e. wrongful imprisonment. Do you wish to change your plea?"

"No, sir. I am as guilty now as I was when arrested."

Very well. Now, on your behalf, do any of you have any statements to offer in mitigation or in defense of the crimes you have confessed to before I consider sentencing you? I have read your statements and find ample evidence to throw the book at you."

Counsel Fromberg began, "May it please the court, your honor. I would like to point out that we have three valued citizens of our community here. Mr. Tyler's charity to the poor as the proprietor of a grocery store for the past 30 years is known far and wide. The other two defendants have served us all with distinction in long and esteemed careers in law enforcement. We owe debts of gratitude to each and every one for their unwavering commitments to us all as model citizens.

"Secondly, your honor, the charges against these defendants arise solely out of their own confessions. We have no victims to testify against them and the investigators of these crimes have no leads to other witnesses that might be implicated in this matter. We need not find reasons to impeach these defendants or deliver them into the harshest of punishments for their actions. They are willing to pay the price for their mistakes and have come here to accept your judgment of them. But I submit, your honor, that these are not the dark and evil criminals that customarily come before your court. These three defendants have been role models, if not martyrs, to us all in the ways in which they have dedicated and conducted their lives in our community. They stand at your mercy now, and I hope your judgment of them will be merciful.

"Thank you, your honor."

"Thank you Mr. Fromberg. Now, does the prosecution have anything to say on this matter?"

"Jeremy Knowles, your honor. May it please the court, the people of the United States deserve recognition by this court of the fundamentals of life and liberty and the fact that there is virtually no life without liberty. To have one's liberty unlawfully taken away is one of the most egregious of crimes and one that deserves the harshest kind of punishment. Your judgment of these defendants should serve as a notice to anyone who might seek to abuse another's liberty, that such actions will be given the severest punishment our statutes can provide.

"I realize there are no victims here as complaining witnesses, but the people stand to seek justice for them the same as we do for homicide victims whose remains are not found. We do not know who the victims of these three men's acts were, nor do we know whether or not they are alive or dead. We don't know for sure that Jeep Rogers was not one of the number of people criminally incarcerated in this scheme, but we do know that he disappeared without a trace after landing in Montana a couple of weeks ago and is still missing. We have the testimony of the three defendants to explain that only they were involved. Really! How many others have taken part in this plot that these men did not implicate? How can we be certain that justice will be served in this matter?

"The people believe that these defendants should be incarcerated for terms that are at least the medium range for their crimes, in spite of their standing as good citizens. Unless we make such a statement to the public, it could be interpreted that our basic rights are in grave peril in our courts.

"Thank you, your honor."

"Very well. I thank both of you and the investigating officers for their work on bringing this case forward and the highly professional manner in which you have managed it.

"Since the time of your arraignments, I have had time to consider the seriousness of the crimes with which the defendants are charged. I have scrutinized in detail the statements of both the prosecution and defense and have determined that no additional time is necessary in which to deliberate on sentencing. Do any of the defendants have anything to say before I pass sentence?"

"No, your honor."

"Therefore, I now ask Mr. Franklin Scott Meador to rise and face the court. Mr. Meador, as to the seven charges of felony wrongful imprisonment, to which you have plead guilty, I hereby sentence you to serve a period of three years in a federal detention facility on each count. As to the seven charges of criminal conspiracy, to which you have plead guilty, I hereby sentence you to a period of three years in a federal detention facility on each count, with such sentence to run concurrently with the aforementioned.

"Mr. Thomas Lincoln Kelly, please rise and face the court. Mr. Kelly, as to the seven charges of felony wrongful imprisonment, to which you have pleaded guilty, I hereby sentence you to serve a period of three years in a federal detention facility on each count. As to the seven charges of criminal conspiracy, to which you have plead guilty, I hereby sentence you to a period of three years in a federal detention facility on each count, with such sentence to run concurrently with the aforementioned.

"Mr. Ruben James Tyler, please rise and face the court. Mr. Tyler, you have admitted guilt to a singular charge of felony conspiracy in this matter and I hereby sentence you to a period of confinement of three years in a federal detention facility for that crime.

"The court recognizes the fact that these are the first offenses ever charged against the defendants and the court further takes serious note that they have individually occupied lengthy careers as stalwart and exemplary citizens of their community. Therefore, it is further ordered and decreed by this court that the sentences herein imposed upon defendants Tyler, Kelly and Meador be suspended and that such suspension will remain in effect for the length of time accorded to each sentence. It is further ordered that the suspension of said sentences will be revoked at such time that any one of the defendants is found in violation of the law. The defendant will then be immediately incarcerated and begin serving the sentence hereby imposed, with time reduced by any period of time already served in detention.

"Defendants are to be supplied by the Clerk of Court with written rules of conduct applicable to the suspended sentences and such rules are hereby made a part of this decree.

"It is further ordered that the entirety of the Old Territorial Prison be kept open to public view in such manner that the safety of visitors is paramount and that inspection of any part thereof shall be immediately granted upon request by any citizen. The U.S. Marshal shall take responsibility for implementing this order and shall remain in charge of the facility until newly appointed local management is in place, subject to the approval of this court.

"So ordered. Court adjourned!"

As the judge rapped his gavel, Janet took note of the glint of gold on the judge's right little finger that briefly reflected the light of the courtroom.

"Whew!" she gasped, "Less than a slap on the hands. The farce is now all wrapped up, never to be an issue again."

At a late lunch, Charles tried to ease Janet's frustrations over the outcome of the case. "Charles, I am livid with disgust over this miscarriage of justice! I know we didn't have much evidence going in, but what if someday Jeep Rogers is found?"

"Janet, we had to do something to prove or disprove your allegations. I have no doubt that you saw what you saw, the evidence simply wasn't there, and today's judgment is virtually a 'case closed' issue. If someday Jeep Roger's body turns up and there is proof through DNA that he was once incarcerated in the old prison, all the accused would have to do is say, 'oh yeah, I remember him, he was one of the prisoners.' Unfortunately, they can't be tried again because of the law of double jeopardy.

"I know this doesn't put your frustrations to rest, but frankly, I don't think you should bother with it anymore."

There was no reply from Janet. The two finished their lunch without further conversation.

CHAPTER 11

Tennessee Tourist

Ashford Lee Keller knew in his teenage years that a career in politics would be his source of lasting wealth, power and fame. His unspoken philosophy dictated that once one learned the inroads of the political establishment and used them to the fullest extent, the exercise of greed, dominance, deceit, coercion and patronage could all be wrapped up under the banner of "patriotism". Adopting Lyndon Baines Johnson as his icon and role model, he had by age 51 garnered almost total penetration of the democrat establishment from his home state of Tennessee to Washington, D.C.

Having served two terms as U.S. Senator, Keller had a year previously completed a full term as Secretary of Agriculture in the previous democrat administration and had set the national financial and political wheels in motion to make a bid for the White House. In a marriage that was without children and no more than a pantomime of togetherness for publicity, Keller had managed to convey the image of marital loyalty and commitment. But it was a carefully engineered pretense that had a lengthy history of upheavals, estrangement and dozens of cases of infidelity on his part. With a great deal of political clout and intimidation, he had managed to keep most of his private life from being fodder for the press and out of public view.

So it had been up until the time he returned to Tennessee from Washington, D.C., some 18 months ago. Discreetly, he also moved his mistress and former staff assistant, 23 year-old Jamie Rae Knight, to a comfortable apartment near his campaign headquarters in Nashville. He was completely taken with her passion, her gullibility and ability to keep their affair a guarded secret. He had everything working for him, and he tackled campaign preparations with new vigor and zeal. Keller was becoming the prominent "favorite son" of the National Democrat Party.

Then something occurred that changed it all. Within two months of their arrival in Nashville, Jamie Rae disappeared without a trace. She left her apartment one afternoon with nothing more than her wallet and keys, spoke to friend who passed her by on the street and then simply disappeared. She had made one phone call to her mother in Georgia on the day she disappeared, and her absence was not reported until nearly two weeks after she had last been seen in front of her apartment building.

Police investigation ensued and her affair with Secretary Keller was blared out all over the national press and television. The story carried on for months and no clues to Jamie Rae's whereabouts were ever discovered. The only element of controversy surfaced in the last telephone conversation she had had with her mother. She revealed to her mother that she had been involved with a wonderful and very influential man who had made commitments to her about a future together. Jamie had told her mother she thought she was pregnant and hoped to have good news about her future to report later.

Speculation swirled around Keller's involvement with the young woman and the possibility that she was pregnant. She was also of the wrong color to be a fitting spouse for the former cabinet official who was on his way to campaigning for President of the United States. Jamie Rae's condition, her race and her background were all serious threats to his carefully crafted public image, thereby presenting more than enough motive for him to have her conveniently "disappear". Keller had a bundle of witnesses and alibis to account for his time and whereabouts on the day she was considered to be missing and no evidence of a crime was ever found. As time passed, the authorities finally classified Jamie Rae as "missing and presumed dead".

Whatever political aspirations and fantasies might have been envisioned by Keller had now faded into rubble as a result of the controversy. For several months he tried every conceivable means of damage control and the resurrection of his political position but everything failed. Publicly he remained the prime suspect in the disappearance of Jamie Rae Knight and nothing he could say would convince anyone otherwise. After a year of being haunted by the press and taunted by others, Keller decided to make himself temporarily scarce in Tennessee, although he had been admonished by the police not to leave the area without letting them know of his plans and whereabouts.

Keller had ancestors who had moved to the Montana Territory after the Civil War, seeking opportunities for new land and commerce in the wake of the Western Gold Rush era. He had heard that some of them had settled near the second territorial capitol of Virginia City, Montana, and he decided that if he could get there secretly, perhaps he might find a quiet place in which to retire from public life and recover some of his privacy. He made a quiet call to the Chief of Detectives of the Nashville Police, received permission to make the trip to Montana and quickly set about making the arrangements. He later reported his travel plans for a flight to Helena and an itinerary of a three or four day stay that would take him to the virtual ghost towns of Virginia City, Nevada City, and Bannack.

After a lengthy but pleasant drive southward from Helena, Keller reached the main street of Virginia City and parked in front of an ornate, old brick building bearing a large, black on white sign, "BAR OF JUSTICE SALOON Marshal Henry Lowell, Proprietor". Strolling up the board walk in his direction was a tall, lanky man wearing a black Stetson hat, badge, western attire and Colt Peacemaker revolver on his right hip. Keller opened his car door, stepped out and was just beginning to stand when the man greeted him, "Hello there, stranger. What brings you to these here parts?"

"Hello, Mister Lawman. I came up here from Tennessee to see if I could trace out some of my ancestors who migrated to Montana mining camps in the early days." Keller had a bit of a puzzled look on his face as he continued, "I know this place is just like time has passed it by for maybe a hundred years or so, but are you involved with making a western movie here or what?"

Chuckling, Pickett responded, "Nope, this is my usual garb. I'm the Sheriff of this county, and I'm very familiar with all these little old ghost towns out here. Come on in to the saloon and I will set up some refreshments, then we can visit about your ancestors."

They entered the bar and found the bartender in quiet conversation with the only other occupant who was sitting with his back to them. "Hey, Henry," Pickett said, "set us up a couple of Jim Backs for me and this visitor here."

As the bartender produced and filled the two glasses, Keller and Pickett took seats at the bar to the right of the other patron. "Mr. Secretary, I want you to meet the proprietor of this here fine establishment, retired U.S. Marshall Henry Lowell."

Lowell spoke but was suddenly interrupted by Keller. In a gasp, he inquired, "Uh . . . sheriff, how do you know who I am?"

Ignoring his question, Pickett then introduced the other man at the bar as a long time friend and fellow lawman, Timberline County Sheriff Brigham Johnson. Johnson, also attired in a Stetson and dark western jacket, slowly turned to face Keller. He raises his glass in toast fashion, "How do, Mr. Secretary. Here's one to yah."

Keller almost dropped his drink. He shuddered as he studied the face to his left and barely choked out his reply, "What in hell is this? Why, you are the spitting image of me! Except for the western stuff, it's almost like looking into a mirror!"

"Haw haw haw," yelped Pickett, "dead ringer sure as hell!" We really got it right finding you a stand in up here didn't we Mr. Secretary? So now I guess I have to answer up to your question. We knew you were coming up here by way of law enforcement in Tennessee. Seems like you are a 'person of interest' down there. We had little time to arrange this little welcoming committee for you but struck it lucky being able to use Brig here. He has taken a lot of B.S. from folks over the "past year 'cause he looks like every TV and newspaper picture of you. Haw haw . . . I guess this will be a right good joke on everyone and he can get even now."

"What do you mean 'joke'?", sputtered Keller. "What is the meaning of all of this? I have noticed that you all wear the same little pinkie ring so this must be some kind of fraternity or old school buddy charade you have cooked up. I fail to get the humor, sheriff."

"Oh, these?" said Lowell, holding up his right little finger. "Why these are only little tokens of part ownership in this here establishment. "Montana gold, Montana Yogo sapphires and the initials 'JB' meaning Jim Beam society. I gave them out to everyone who made an investment in this place and they can have any kind of Jim Beam drink in here, on the house, when ever they want it, forever, long as they show this ring."

"Well," continued Pickett, "Here's the way it all works out, Mr. Secretary. The whole goddamned planet knows you are guilty as hell of getting rid of that pretty little Jamie Rae Knight. No physical or eyewitness evidence, but you are buried under a mountain of means, MOTIVE and opportunity, and we are here to serve justice for her."

"There has been no evidence implicating me, no proof, no arrest and sure as hell no indictment of any kind! If you are trying to scare or intimidate me into making some kind of plea or confession, forget it! I am innocent of anything to do with her disappearance and that's it! It didn't work, boys, and now I am leaving. Thanks for the drink."

From behind him, Johnson spoke in a low voice, almost a growl, "I don't think you will be leaving right off, Mr. Secretary. The three of us have enough pistol lead here to weight you down kinda heavily before you get through those doors. Maybe you had better just calm down and listen a piece. Enjoy the rest of your drink too 'cause you won't be tasting much of that from here on out."

"Mr. Secretary, I am going to make this as official and clear to you as possible", said Pickett. "A committee of ten men, all honorable citizens of experience in the law, have met and deliberated on your case at great length, almost continually night and day for the past two days. From newspaper and television accounts, testimony against you has been weighed and judged, and an advocate speaking in your behalf has been present at each and every session. That court has found you guilty of responsibility for the disappearance of Jamie Rae Knight and has sentenced you to life in prison without parole. I am taking you into custody here and now, and will carry out that sentence."

"This cannot be happening!" Keller choked. "There has been no trial, I have had no counsel, there is no way this is real! You have had your fun at my expense so now just let it be and I will be on my way."

Johnson spoke again. "This is no joke, Mr. Secretary. I will be returning your rental car to Helena and flying your tickets back to Nashville. Somewhere down there 'you' will disappear and no one will have a clue as to what happened to you or where you are, just like Jamie Rae. Now you best get shuck of that jacket and tie, and give me all of your I.D., tickets and car keys. You won't be needing cash where you're going either, so hand it over too. Damn! I guess I will have to shed my boots for those sissy shoes you're wearing."

Pickett emphasized, "Right Brig. Mr. Keller, you do exactly what he just said and do it right now! If we have to use force, we would be thoroughly delighted."

As Keller nervously complied, he screeched, "You have the upper hand on this prank right now but I swear to get even! No way in hell you will get away with this!"

"Take it easy Keller," said the bartender. "You are going to see a little bit more of colorful, old-time Montana between here and Bannack. Enjoy it while you can, that jail up there is kinda small and has no windows in it."

Within minutes, he was escorted out the back door of the saloon to Pickett's cruiser. They parted company with Johnson, and the journey to Bannack began.

CHAPTER 12

Investment Certificate

Bannack, Montana

For Charles and Janet, the move from Montana to a permanent home in Olympia, Washington, had been an exhausting, hectic four weeks. Now situated in a spacious brick, split-level overlooking Puget Sound, they were well into their final unpacking chores. From one of the boxes labeled, "Master Bedroom", Janet brought out Charles' jewelry box, casually taking note of its contents of tie tacks, cuff links, some old coins and lapel trivia of law enforcement origins. "Charles, what is this curious little ring with the blue stone and the initials 'JB'? It sure seems familiar to me but I can't recall just where I have seen it. I have never seen you wearing it before, have I?"

"Oh, that," he replied. "Well, it's kind of a symbol of ownership in a little old saloon in Virginia City, Montana. A number of years ago, an old friend, Henry Lowell, retired from the U.S. Marshal Service and wanted to open up a bar there. He needed money and offered up shares of ownership in the place to anyone in law enforcement who would invest $500, and in return he gave each one of those little rings. That became the 'Bar of Justice Saloon' and I guess he still runs the place. Anyhow, it's a nice little trinket that has some value. You see, the 'JB' stands for Jim Beam society and anyone wearing the ring can have any drink made from Jim Beam, on the house, forever."

"That's a great idea for financing. No wonder I found it somewhat familiar. I probably have seen lots of law and order people wearing it."

"Yes, I'll bet he has gotten upwards of 1,500 people invested in that place and it truly was a good idea. I'm happy to be a member. By the way, and speaking of Virginia City, gossip in the Bureau says that former Ag Secretary, Ashford Keller recently made a visit up there and completely disappeared after he returned to Nashville. Not a single trace of where he might be, and they are under real pressure from the press to find him."

Janet mused, "Wow! Disappeared just like that mistress he is suspected of abducting. Maybe he and she are secretly rejoined somewhere and living happily ever after. Or maybe he stumbled into the Bar of Justice out there and is keeping company with Jeep Rogers. One could never be sure about any of that, right?"

PART II

The Well of Justice

CHAPTER 13

The Galloping Gallows of Montana

Before the state took over the process of carrying out the death penalty in Montana, responsibility for those events began with the vigilantes and later became the chores of individual county sheriffs. A sentence of death by hanging was the official method of execution. In the mid-1940's the Montana attorney general was made painfully aware of the necessity for the state to come up with a uniform mechanism for handling death sentences after a couple of somewhat botched hangings took place in Missoula County.

The outrage of the press over those incidents brought pressure to bear on the governor, and he directed the attorney general to come up with a uniform, effective and portable means of administering death sentences. Such an approved mechanism would be available for the use of any county court and would be of such construction that future criticism could be avoided.

The attorney general arranged for a Helena mechanical engineer to come up with blueprints for a gallows that could be easily assembled and taken down, so that it could be conveniently transported to any county in the state that had need of it. With the next hanging due soon, again in Missoula County, there was not a lot of time to spare in getting an "officially approved" gallows constructed and on its way there.

A longtime Missoula County Assessor was a witness to the two events in Missoula that led up to the need for a portable gallows. Here's the way he described the origins of Missoula County's gallows design:

"Well, I watched them all from my office here on the second floor where this window faces out to the west lawn beside the old jail there. The first one was back in 1939, as I recollect. The county had gotten away from using hanging trees by then and was determined to carry out executions with some kind of civility and dignity. However, the commissioners did not see a need for erecting a costly gallows platform with trap door and such, so they asked the county engineer to come up with a plan for a less costly method of getting on with a humane, clean hanging.

"So, the engineer made up some blue prints for the damnedest contraption I ever saw. It was a couple of A-frames braced upright, and on top of them, a fulcrum beam supported a lengthy pole, mounted on axles. The long end of the pole held the rope and noose, and a barrel of rocks was suspended off the short end for a counterweight. A suspension rope held the main beam almost level and was tethered to a snubbing bolt by a slipknot. It was a kind of cantilever affair that could be easily assembled without need for stairs, a platform or trapdoor. The way he had it figured was that once assembled out on the lawn, the prisoner could be led up close under the beam and stand there until the noose was fixed up. Then the sheriff could pull the slipknot and the lever would jerk the noose upward and instantly break the neck of the condemned.

"The commissioners asked the treasurer and me what we thought, and we told them that it looked like it might work. So they had the thing built and tested it with a bag of sand. It must have worked out okay, so they put the rig away until the day before the hanging.

"For the execution day, they built a tall board fence around part of the lawn out there to keep little kids from watching the goings-on, and on this side of it, they erected the cantilever gallows thing. It was right down there, below my window. On the day of the execution, the official witnesses were let in, along with the county coroner, and a number of spectators gathered around. Must have been about a hundred folks or so, including peace officers. At the appointed time, the sheriff and one of his deputies brought the prisoner out of the old jail there and led him into the enclosure where he was positioned under the cantilever beam. His hands were already manacled behind his back and his belt was used to bind his ankles. I couldn't hear if anything was said before they placed a black hood over his head and adjusted the noose around his neck.

"The sheriff stepped back to the side of the A-frame where he grabbed the tether rope. After a couple of seconds, he gave it a stout jerk and the cantilever whipped upward in a flash as the barrel of rocks hit the ground. The force jerked the prisoner off the lawn and snapped him upward like a bass plug on the end of a casting rod. Hell! Next thing I knew, here he was, right there outside my window, upside down with the rope around his neck!

"He fell back down to the grass, near where he had stood, thrashing and bucking and going through an awful mess. The coroner rushed up and exclaimed, 'Sheriff! If we can get this man across the street to my office, I think I can save him!' The sheriff sez, 'Aye, Gawd, Bob, you touch that guy and I'll shootcha! Court sez he was to hang by the neck until dead! Still got the rope around his neck and ain't dead yet, so you just back off!'

"The sheriff calmly lit a cigar as they paused to wait a few minutes until the prisoner lay still on the ground. He then said, 'Okay, Bob, he looks kinda dead by now, so do your duty and pronounce him.' The coroner moved in, put a stethoscope to the man's chest and said, 'Yep, he's dead, sheriff.' The sheriff made a note of the date and time on his court papers, told everyone it was over and asked them to leave. The next day, the Hellgate Daily News had a fit about how barbaric this execution had been, writing columns on all the horrid details. The sheriff found himself in one helluva political mess and wasn't able to explain anything to the satisfaction of his critics. Best he could do was blame the commissioners and the county engineer.

"Well, the noise came up all over again a couple of years later when another hanging was scheduled in Missoula. The sheriff was up for re-election, and he went about reassuring everyone that he was not going to be blamed for creating a circus like he did on the other one. 'This will be handled like any regular hanging with a trap door and everything, and damned if there is going to be a big bunch of witnesses and press muttering around about this one, either!', he said. 'We are going to handle this job right, and inside the jail house where there ain't enough room for a herd of spectators.'

"The sheriff planned it all out very thoroughly. The old, three-story jail had his office and the galley on the first floor, men's cells on the second, and the women's jail on the third floor. He arranged to have a square hole about three feet on a side cut through the floor in the corridor area between the third and second floors. He then had a trapdoor installed, with a spring latch on the bottom, which could be released by pulling a chain. He made sure to limit the onlookers to only three official witnesses, the coroner and one reporter from the <u>Hellgate Daily News</u> whom he trusted to be fair about the whole event. Being an elected official, he needed the press, but not the kind of hostile reporting he had born the brunt of on the last hanging.

"On the execution day, a couple of dozen curious folks and reporters milled around outside the jail house while the sheriff went about his business inside. He had a deputy handcuff the prisoner on the second floor and escort him upstairs to the women's area. There weren't any women in jail at the time, so none had to be moved around. When they got to the area of the trapdoor, the deputy told the prisoner to stand on it while his ankles were buckled together. The hood was then placed and the noose adjusted. The prisoner asked, 'So, how does this thing work?' The deputy told him, 'The sheriff is downstairs ready to pull a latch that will release the trapdoor and you go on from there to meet your Maker.' 'Okay, but how will the sheriff know when I'm ready?' 'Cause I'm gonna yell at him, that's how,' said the deputy, whereupon the prisoner yells, 'Hey sheriff! Let 'er rip!' The sheriff pulled the latch and 'thump', the prisoner fell to a merciful death.

"Next day, the <u>Hellgate Daily News</u> had big fat headlines: 'Condemned Man Carries Out His Own Execution!' Oh boy! The sheriff caught hell again for that one! This time the governor was put on the spot and had to come up with a solid solution. As well, the sheriff lost the election that year. Too bad 'cause he was a pretty good sheriff in spite of it all.

"So that was why the state came up with the galloping gallows idea and, along about 1945 or so, we were the first to use it. It was a good setup with a wood frame all put together with big carriage bolts. Had a platform, overhead beam for the rope and a trapdoor that could be sprung by pulling a handle. Looked just like the ones you see in the western movies, except it could be taken down and trucked from one place to another. It worked just fine for the last hanging we had here, and that was the last execution handled by any county. The state is in charge of all those things now. Problem is, no one seems to know where the galloping gallows went.

"When the new annex was built here, all of the county shops and storage spaces were shuffled around and the galloping gallows weren't found anywhere. I saw them disassembled by a county crew and one of the guys said they were set aside for shipping to the territory prison at Scribner. When the old prison was shut down, another hunt went on for the gallows, but they never turned up there, either. I have heard rumors that maybe one outfit knows where they are, but they have a lot of secrets.

"It's the Justice Brigade, a kind of a closed, elite bunch of law enforcement from around the state, and no one knows how many there are or exactly how to get in touch with them. Too bad. The gallows are a colorful old relic of our history."

Missoula County cantilever gallows, c-1939.

CHAPTER 14

Lotus-Eater, Ph.D.

Arleigh Smith was the spoiled product of a wealthy, socially pretentious family of Portland, Oregon. He spent his youth and his parents' money on marijuana and years of random, meaningless education to avoid service in the U.S. military during the war in Viet Nam. He specialized in protests, pot, civil disobedience, and general obstruction of "the system." Excepting for his circle of like-minded social rejects, he was a misfit whose only prescription for a future was to preserve his accustomed lifestyle perpetually. At some point in time, he aroused enough energy to scramble his disjointed array of collegiate credits into a degree in ecology, as so many over-the-hill hippies have done, and he ultimately earned a doctorate in that discipline.

With family money abused to exhaustion, and having matriculated to a higher level of student sludge, a new realization somehow penetrated his clouded mind with the startling awareness that he might have to choose a new survival venue to replace the risky economics of drug-dealing and lounging around the Oregon state campus. He would also require fertile turf in which his cultural outlook could take roots, a place not yet aware of the dynamics of people living in filth who could make their rewards by attacking the mainstream's abuse of the pristine cleanliness of raw nature.

Those ambitions were certain to draw him like a magnetic force to Missoula, Montana, as it had done with numbers of the hippie generation whose influences had overtaken a good part of the University of Montana campus. For him, Missoula was a new, naïve frontier in which he could again flourish as a leader of protests, maintain himself as a consumer and dealer in illegal drugs and continue to lounge around on a college campus. With new visions of success rattling around in his head, Arleigh gathered up his two live-in girlfriends and their three children from the hovel they inhabited in downtown Portland, and migrated eastward over the mountains to their new "Shangri-La" in Missoula. There he became an icon to the transplanted, bathless subculture of the university liberal crowd, while cherishing the fantasy that he might someday come into contact with his idol, Jane Fonda.

Smith first registered a non-profit group under the name of PUFIN (People United for Forests and Indivisible Nature) and, over several years, invaded newspaper headlines and television with protests against any conceivable use of natural resources for the benefit of mankind. PUFIN was an amalgam of special interests such as PETA, Friends of the Wilderness, Handgun Control, Inc., and the Sierra Club. The youthful zealots of the university law school were enthusiastic contributors of petitions and legal filings that Smith used in various courts to block investments in vital industries or impair earnest labor in farms, forests, small mines and essential urban developments throughout the state.

By exercising his visibility, he could garner local financial contributions on any given day he might threaten to file another of his endless complaints over the pollution caused by the exhausts of diesel trucks on the interstate highway or the Smurfitt-Stone pulp mill in nearby Frenchtown.

Among his followers, he flaunted his reputation for being the source of many victories throughout the state, having driven three lumber mills into bankruptcy, along with hosts of loggers, truckers and heavy equipment operators. He boasted of 12 ranchers being driven off their places by nuisance environmental court orders, and having their ancestral properties sold off cheaply to "preservation" interests. In recent times, PUFIN's most dramatic ventures involved dispersing its members during hunting season into all corners of the state to physically disrupt and harass hunters in their quests for wild turkeys, deer, elk and waterfowl. Trout fishermen had also been recently added to their list of victims.

One of the least known, but saddest, of PUFIN's spoilings involved retired Bozeman policeman, Ben Archer. Archer, a widower, never remarried and used a major portion of his retirement savings to improve upon a small patented gold mining property he had acquired in the remote backcountry of the Crazy Mountains. He had built a comfortable cabin for himself, with added room for his children's and grandchildren's occasional summer visits. A water well was drilled and the premises housed a costly, but very modern septic system and power plant. His yield of gold from the sparse, thin little veins in hard quartzite was far less than could have repaid the time and expense of labor given to chipping it out, running it through a small mill, and carrying the proceeds to Butte for sale. But his was not a venture for grand riches. He enjoyed the test of his abilities to survive, refreshed each day with the unspoiled natural environment and the colorful history of the Montana he loved.

Somehow, Arleigh Smith heard about Ben Archer, the prospector, and began with a vengeance to have him stopped from extracting another trace of gold. His goal was to force his removal from the Crazy Mountains for good. Archer was a fourth-generation Montanan and those were the people whom Smith had come to loathe. Native Montanans never seemed to recognize the benefits of his leadership or his selfless attitude about defending their beloved state. He resented their disdain for him and his followers, and he sought every opportunity to prove to the "unenlightened ones" that he could not be ignored. The opportunity to attack Ben Archer ideally suited his purpose. Reciting a plethora of state anti-pollution and mining ordinances, Smith and his legal advisors put together a "cease and desist" petition and filed it against Archer in state court in Bozeman.

It was all accomplished without anyone from PUFIN ever setting foot on his property to verify their claims or even finding his diggings on a map. Archer was compelled to stop all work on his property until the state mining and environmental authorities could examine every detail of his operation, mine safety and hazards, waste materials handling, proceeds, septic system, surface water degradation and any removal of natural topsoil and vegetation. In order for him to avoid eviction from his claims and private residence, Archer would have to hire an attorney and employ any number of environmental and chemical consultants. Of course, he was financially unable to do any of that.

On his last visit to the Butte assay office, Archer joined the proprietor and longtime friend for a cup of coffee. He placed a used, clean olive jar filled with fine jagged wires of native gold onto the table. Through the side of the slender little glass bottle, Ben could see the polished sides of a large milled nugget. He smiled, knowing that his friend would later discover a faceted, half-carat Yogo sapphire buried in the tiny yellow filaments. "Carl, gimme a buck for this."

"What do you mean, 'a buck', Ben? You know that gold is worth about four hundred, at least."

"Nope, I want a buck and will give you a bill of sale for it right here and now, Carl. This is the last of the millings I will be bringing in here and I want you to have it. I'm closing down my little diggings and will be making camp elsewhere, I reckon. Not sure where, right now," said Archer.

"Well, sorry to hear that, Ben. We've been good friends for years and I hope you can stay in these parts. Anything you need, just call on me."

"Give me one of your receipt slips, Carl." After tearing the top one from the pad, Archer carefully dated it and wrote, "Sold this date to Carl Thornburg one olive jar of rough gold for one dollar and other valuable considerations. Your friend forever, Benjamin Archer."

"Now, I need to use your restroom, Carl, and then I'll be on my way."

Shortly after Ben had disappeared to the rear of the office, Thornburg heard the crack of a gunshot and ran to the restroom where he found Ben Archer dead from a large gushing wound to his right temple.

Arleigh Smith heard about Archer's suicide because it resulted in PUFIN's lawsuit being suspended. He gloated over the victory with his coterie of aging flower children and promised they would ferret out every spoiler of the wilderness and give them the same treatment until all of their kind would be unable to access the land. A number of other Montanans took notice of Archer's loss as well. They were law enforcement members of the Justice Brigade and Ben Archer had been one of them.

Within a few weeks of Archer's burial, a Missoula police detective accosted Smith late one Thursday afternoon.

"Hey, Arleigh, I have some serious news for you. I hear there are four or five out-of-work loggers from Darby coming to town looking for you, and they seem to be out for blood. They know where you live and, if I were you, I would high tail it out of town right away and spend the weekend out of sight. We should be able to intercept them and send them home by then."

"Well, officer, I have kids in school and won't be able to just pick everything up and leave any time I might be threatened. Your job is to protect my family and me, so I guess you can handle that kind of trouble, right?"

"We are paid by the taxpayers, sonny," replied the detective. "I don't think you have paid a penny of taxes in your whole life, so you wouldn't really expect us to give you a lot of concern, would you? Besides, I don't believe there is any threat to your food stamps, or your wives and kids, so why don't you just go away for a couple of days and let this thing blow itself out?"

"Okay, cop, I get the message. You won't do your duty, so I have to get out of town. You are a real disgrace to your profession, you know that? I have a bunch of lawyers who will take you on for harassing me this way. Think about that and your retirement!"

"Adios, doctor Smith, you filthy bastard! Hit the road right now and just make sure you don't show up around here for a few days."

Within an hour, Smith was on his way out of Missoula, headed toward the upper Blackfoot River and one of several hippie communal villages where he often hung out. At about 8:00 p.m., a highway patrolman, parked off the highway on a graveled Blackfoot National Forest access road, saw the 1979, rusted-out maroon Peugeot cross his vision from right to left. He quickly brought his cruiser in behind the Peugeot with his emergency lights on and the car ahead came to a stop on the roadside. Keying his radio microphone, he reported, "Twenty six to base. ID on Peugeot, tag four, papa, zebra, three, one, one, kilo. Copy?"

A female voice crackled over the speaker, repeating the message as the patrolman stepped onto the pavement and cautiously approached the stopped vehicle. As the driver rolled his window down, the odor of rotting caked dreadlocks mingled with the unmistakable stench of marijuana and wafted out to foul the clean night air.

"Good evening, sir. Please turn your ignition off and hand me your keys. I need to see your driver's license, registration and insurance card."

"What in hell are you stopping me for? I haven't done anything wrong and don't need to turn my engine off. If you are going to ticket me, just do it and I will be going where I want to."

From the parked cruiser another voice spoke, "Hey, Jim, it's the professor all right. Dispatch is still reading from a long list of misdemeanor arrests, multiple drug busts, resisting, unlawful assembly, trespass, assault and more of the same."

The patrolman spoke again. "You shut that engine off right now and give me you're goddamned keys, sir!" As he complied, the officer continued, "Okay, doc, just open the door and get out of that little pile of junk. Keep your hands in sight, you hear? Do it, right now! Come to the rear of the car and take the position. I'm sure you know what that is, right?"

Smith came out of the car muttering curses, adding words about harassment and pigs.

"I have to inspect your car, sir. Do you have any guns or drugs in your possession?" He was then joined by the other officer who assisted with a body frisk and handcuffed Smith's hands behind his back.

"Guns? I don't believe anyone should have guns, not even you! No, I don't have guns or drugs on me, so get the cuffs off!"

Emerging from the driver's side of the Peugeot, the patrolman held a ziplock bag of dark granular material into the cruiser's headlights.

"Well, now, professor, what do you call this little package, a baloney sandwich? I found it stuffed behind the cushion on the passenger side of your car. Seems like you were the only one in there, so in our happy little game of tag, YOU'RE IT! Ha-ha-ha!"

"I don't know whose that is or how it got there. It's not mine and I deny having possession. I think you planted it there in order to bag me and you will be in big trouble for that!"

The patrolman busied himself between the two cars, filling out a form in his citation book. "Ok, doc, just to show you what generous, wonderful cops we are, I have left the pot off the ticket here and have written you for only that bad right tail light and not having your seatbelt on. I will remove your cuffs so that you can sign it and our game warden friend here will put the grass back where I found it. Fair deal?"

"Okay, I'll go for that, but I still think you guys have my number and are harassing me at every turn."

With that, Smith's handcuffs were removed and he leaned over the back of his car to sign the citation. The game warden opened the passenger side of the Peugeot and apparently returned the plastic bag to the place where it had been discovered.

"Now, doc, we have to replace your handcuffs and get you into the back of my cruiser here. Your car is unsafe to drive at night and will have to remain where we can watch it so that it won't get vandalized any more than it already is."

As he flipped the owner's keys to the game warden, he continued, "We will follow along behind the warden in your car until he finds a secure parking place. Hate to have to put you in here 'cause it will probably take me a week to get the stench out."

Still gasping with anger, Smith replied, "Well, what about me? Where in hell are you going to take me? I was going to camp out around here for a few days, so what do you plan to do about that, huh?"

The Peugeot moved onto the pavement ahead of them in a cloud of oily smoke and the cruiser eased in to keep pace behind it. The patrolman again checked in with his dispatcher, "Twenty-six here, wrote citation golf twenty-niner oh, two, eighty seven. Faulty taillight and no seat belt. Stop made at Bear Creek intersection."

"Ten four, twenty-six. Golf twenty-nine, oh, two, eighty-seven. Dispatch, bye."

The patrolman continued, "Base, I'm turning around here to head back to the other leg of my beat at Seeley Lake."

The dispatcher acknowledged as he continued to follow the Peugeot.

"I got the word from Missoula that you were a little testy when you learned that our law enforcement people wouldn't fall all over themselves trying to protect you from that pack of Darby loggers. So, consider this another favor. I am taking you into protective custody so that you won't get all banged up like you deserve."

"You can't do that! You are violating my civil rights and the whole damned bunch of you will get fired over this mess, probably go to jail!"

"Listen up here real good, professor. You are not black and, therefore, you have no civil rights! Keep a lock on your lips or you will sure as hell find out how few rights you really have right now. You are maggot-infested vermin and deserve no more respect than that, so just shut up and take the ride."

"Where will I be held in your 'protective custody' farce? I want your name and badge number, too. Are those your initials, 'J.B.' on that little pinkie ring? Just remember, I will get out of this and come looking for all of you in court!"

The patrolman calmly replied, "You are going to the old jailhouse at Snowshoe, once the county seat of Timberline County before the mines went bust. You have my name and badge number on the citation and, no, those aren't my initials. This ring identifies me as a part of what we call the 'Jim Beam' society," he chuckled. "Kind of like a stock certificate for an investment in a little old Montana bar in Virginia City." Now, shut up and I mean button your lips or I will button them for you!"

The two cars continued eastward on the highway for another 15 miles until they arrived at a gravel road intersection marked, "Fishing Access." As the Peugeot turned into the parking area, its headlights splashed across a parked Ford Explorer bearing a police light bar with markings of the Montana Department of Natural Resources. It was obviously the game warden's vehicle.

"This is where you change ponies, Smith. The game warden will be carrying you on over to Snowshoe tonight and I will try to air out my cruiser on the way back to Seeley Lake."

"Officer, this whole thing has been a planned setup! You picked that warden up before you stopped me and you knew I was coming out this way. What is really going on?"

"Don't bother yourself about details, doc. You aren't going to be attacked by the Darby bunch and that's what you need to be thankful for, right? Make sure you behave on your way to Snowshoe."

At that point, the game warden arrived at the rear passenger door of the cruiser. The two officers escorted Smith to the Explorer and secured him into the back compartment. The patrolman spoke "good night" to them and the two vehicles departed in separate ways.

CHAPTER 15

Den of the Mountain Lions

**Timberline County Courthouse,
Snowshoe, Montana**

The Justice Brigade has a nucleus, but it is as hidden and shadowy as a den of the mountain lions. Late one Thursday evening, a call from the "den" was made to

Sheriff Brigham Johnson of Timberline County at his home in Sacajawea.

The deep, hollow voice spoke, "Greetings brother! We have some work at hand out at Snowshoe. Wanted to know if you could get away tonight and it may last on into tomorrow. If you aren't busy, we need you to chair a committee."

Johnson replied, "Not tied up with anything here that would interfere. I can be out there in about an hour."

"Good. We have a prisoner in custody and a game warden is transporting him. A detective from Missoula is on his way with a big rap sheet on this guy. He will be our prosecutor, and Reamy Nelson from Bigfork will be defense. Three other members will meet you there."

"Happy to oblige. I'll leave right away." There was a click on the phone circuit and the conversation was over.

Johnson was serving his 18th year as sheriff of Timberline County and had been a member of the Justice Brigade for more than 12 years. Timberline County was his birthplace and, from his childhood, he had been fascinated by the mining ghost town of Snowshoe, which was the original county seat when Montana became a state in 1889.

He, his wife, children, and dozens of members of their church, along with law enforcement officers from around the state, had spent many summers rehabilitating the old buildings at Snowshoe. They cleared the town of most of the packrats, piles of refuge, weeds and debris, and replanted shrubbery and grass over the mill wastes. Several old cabins were made livable, and the little fences and gardens around them were restored. They kept the single road into town in good repair and, for safety, had capped a 1,100 foot deep, vertical, mining shaft with concrete, leaving a locked iron manhole in its center for inspections or environmental testing purposes.

The summer days at remote Snowshoe were memorable times of hard work, outdoor picnics, relaxing evenings, and wonderful conversation for everyone. The feature piece of their endeavors was the restoration of the old courthouse and jail. Paint, salvage lumber and a great deal of devoted energy had rebuilt the icon of the old town center to most of its former character and glory. They were very proud of their achievements in Snowshoe and kept it all a secret from outsiders. Snowshoe had become their private Montana ghost town.

As Sheriff Johnson's headlights penetrated the darkness along the familiar mountain road to Snowshoe, his thoughts returned to old familiar questions and fantasies that arose whenever he saw the town or picked up a piece of its antiquity. "If that old place could just talk," he mumbled aloud.

He pulled to the front of the old courthouse where several cars were parked. Through its windows he could see the soft reflections from oil lamps and the faint drift of blue smoke from the chimney above the old iron wood stove. When he stepped from his cruiser, he was met by a game warden returning from the adjacent, 2-cell jailhouse.

"Hello, Brig! I have our guy all locked up in there and I think he will be somewhat comfortable through the night, if he stays calmed down. Far as he knows, he's in protective custody."

"Hi, Bill. Well, that's just fine and I hope we get this thing done without wasting too much time. Looks like the rest of the guys are here already, so maybe we can get started. Make sure you remove all of his personal effects, okay?"

Johnson and the warden entered a warmly lit room with several rows of benches. Near the entrance, a large iron stove crackled with a dancing fire of split pine and tamarack blocks. A wide table stood on a raised dais at the front, surrounded on the far side by six chairs. Glass oil lamps glowed from each side of the table and in the corners of the room. A large black Bible occupied the center of the table, along with an old miner's sampling pick to be used as a gavel. Note pads and pencils were placed at one corner for the use of the members.

"Walt Evans, I see you're here. It's good to see you again. You're handling prosecution, right? And where's our defense counsel, Reamy Nelson?"

Evans spoke, "Yep, I am. We're all here and Reamy is out back for a pause before we get started."

Nelson stood motionless on the back stoop of the darkened building, deeply troubled over what he had learned from the other committee members when he arrived. He inhaled the clean, cool air, wanting to disappear into a pitch-black mountain night. It was not to be, as he first suspected, a business meeting to discuss Brigade activities. This meeting was not even remotely related to such a common task. Instead, he was in Snowshoe to be part of a real and very serious vigilante meeting, convened to deal with a person charged with "treachery."

Nelson had never imagined that such activities involved the Justice Brigade; however, it now would be his job to defend the man in a court he wanted no part of. He had no idea who the defendant was, the nature of his offense, or what his fate might be if found guilty. He could hardly find his breath as he labored with the mental and physical impact of the burden he faced. Nelson could think of no way to question the proceedings, be excused from his responsibility, or request a delay for time to prepare. He would have to go through with the process and determine a course of action later.

Shuddering, Nelson entered the courtroom through the back door and Johnson asked them all to take places at the table. As they were taking their seats, one of the group retrieved a soiled, granite-colored coffeepot that had been simmering on the wood stove, offering tin cups around, which he filled for each. Johnson placed his left hand on the Bible and banged the miner's sampling pick once onto a small, flat block of wood. "God bless America, Montana, this honorable committee and the work we are about to do here tonight. We're in session, so, Mr. Prosecutor, let's get 'er goin'."

With a screeching of chair legs on the wooden floor, Evans got to his feet and shuffled papers together into a manila folder as he slowly walked around the table to face the group.

"The man's name is Arleigh Smith, and he is charged with the crime of treachery. I am here to prove to you that he is guilty of that crime and should suffer whatever punishment this here committee wants to give him. He's a filthy, goddamned pot-head hippy, with a Ph.D. in ecology, who moved to Missoula from Portland about five years ago."

Nelson raised his hand and interrupted, "I object, Mister Chairman. Calling this guy names like that will prejudice anyone here to fairly judge his character or the offense."

"You're right, Nelson," Johnson added. "Evans, cut some slack here about cussin' this guy. We want to be as fair and open to his innocence as to his guilt."

"Ok, Mister Chairman." Evans continued, "He's got two live-in mistresses and three young kids. I have a list of misdemeanor offenses on this guy as long as both your arms, mostly drug busts, obstruction, criminal assembly for leading protests, assault and battery, vandalism, petty theft, rioting, and resisting arrest. That stuff goes all the way back through his teenage years in Oregon. But those are minor offenses that have nothing to do with the seriousness of the treachery he has committed upon this honorable state. They just go along to show what kind of a low-life we are dealing with here.

"From way back when, this 'professor,' Arleigh Smith, has been the backbone of protests against the timber industry, getting into the news headlines by chaining himself to trees in the path of logging operations, vandalizing logging equipment, spiking timber trees and such. I'm passing around to you all a bunch of newspaper clippings from his police files to show how active and destructive he has been. Entire lumbering towns full of good, earnest workers have lost their jobs as a direct result of his leading literally hundreds of young student flower people into his form of treachery.

"After his move to Missoula, he got a loop around a bunch of dingbat, young law students who volunteered to get his dirty work into court. Year after year, they have used and abused Montana's environmental laws by bringing our honored system of justice to bear upon the earnest, hardworking people of our state. He is an anarchist who has reversed the course of our legal framework and poisoned the well of justice. Smith's treachery has resulted in thousands of our workers losing their jobs and being forced from their homes.

"In one case, he took a personal initiative that brought about the suicide of one of our dear friends, Ben Archer.

That Ph.D. took dead center aim at good old Archer and heaped lawsuits on him that no one could possibly contend against. Ben was a caring man who treasured the natural beauty of our state and never did anything to harm it. Smith's malicious lawsuits barred Ben from his own cabin and quiet little diggings in the mountains. Archer loved that place and all he was doing was working a little gold stringer there. He had no means to defend himself, so he committed suicide.

"The charge against Smith is one we must consider most seriously, with a mind to sending a warning to all of his followers and anyone like him who might become such a threat—'Don't mess with the system of right and wrong that we cherish in Montana!'

"That takes care of my piece for now, Brigham. Be happy to answer all of your questions after the defense has its say."

"Thank you, Mr. Evans, for a good presentation. We'll take a short break for a smoke and some coffee before we resume."

Reamy Nelson remained at the table, shuffling through his notes, while the others milled about the room, replenishing their coffee, adding firewood to the stove, and lighting cigarettes. No one spoke about the indictment they had just heard. After a few minutes, they took their places and the chairman called them to order.

"Your turn, Mister Defense, and you had better do your damned level best. We aren't holding a 'kangaroo court' here, you know."

"Your honors, uh, I mean, gentlemen, the worst that Mr. Smith is accused of is gathering together some dissident people who are not happy with the way our laws have allowed the wanton destruction of our environment.

"He assembled volunteers in enough numbers to gain political clout and public attention. Through his leadership, they have taken their grievances into our court system where they belong. We sure as hell can't fault that! It's called 'due process' and that is what we all are sworn to protect for everyone in Montana. His activities could have been violent, but they weren't.

"I want you all to think deeply about this. The founding fathers of this country acted in much more dangerous ways. They met in secret and conspired to overthrow the government and law of the land. We honor those guys as heroes, every one of them, and now we have a man here charged as a criminal for doing things much less serious than they did." Little did he realize the irony of his words.

Evans rose to interject, "Right, Reamy, but the forefathers of this country could have been hauled out and shot by the redcoats anytime they were discovered in such treachery. We have a better system and aim to protect it as much as the British did."

"Go ahead, Mr. Nelson," said Johnson. "Walt, hold on to your comments for the questions and rebuttal part of this session."

Nelson continued, "Gentlemen, this is a simple constitutional issue here. Smith exercised his right of free assembly, but sometimes carried it out of bounds and he got arrested and punished for that. He used his freedom of speech to express his opinions and other people have responded to his message.

"There is nothing criminal about that, either, even though he brought pressure to bear on industries that sometimes caused them financial problems. Train wrecks and fires also cause financial problems, but I don't think many of them can be blamed on protesters.

"As far as him being responsible for the death of Ben Archer, that's stretching things too far! Mr. Archer died of his own hand, and suicide is a very personal thing. Arleigh Smith had no intention of killing Archer and had no part in doing him in. None of us really understand the reasons for suicide, but we know damned sure it isn't murder. This panel has seen no evidence that remotely points to Smith. He is not guilty of murder or treachery to commit murder, and he is not in any way connected with Ben's death.

"With all considered, gentlemen, I say that this committee can go no farther than banish him from Montana so that he can be free to exercise his rights somewhere else. He is not healthy for Montana, and Montana would not be a healthy place for him to remain. I am confident that you will agree with me. That's my appeal to the committee and I am ready to answer your questions."

"Thank you, Mr. Nelson," said the chairman. "In an orderly fashion, we will now ask questions of each side on this matter and both defense and prosecution are free to ask and reply to questions of each other. I will make sure this is kept respectable and in order."

From that point, the arguments and questions continued on into the night until the chairman decided they were treading over ground previously covered. He dismissed both prosecution and defense, asking them to take the prisoner some coffee and wait in the jailhouse until summoned. "When we call, gag and cuff the prisoner and bring him in here," Johnson said.

The remaining five men of the committee then began deliberations on guilt or innocence and method of punishment. As the bright yellow and pink glow of a rich Montana sky began to filter through the quaking aspens and cast shadows across the little village, one of the committee-men came to the step of the old courthouse and yelled in the direction of the adjacent jail, "We're ready. Bring the prisoner."

Nelson and Evans ushered the prisoner forward between them. His hands were manacled behind him and a red paisley, cotton bandana was tied tightly across his mouth.

Struggling, Smith was thrust through the courtroom until he faced the seated committee from a few feet away.

Johnson began, "Mister Ph.D., Arleigh Smith, you are here to answer to the criminal charge of treachery. We have held court on your case and an appointed counsel has duly represented you. Our deliberations have lasted half the night, and we have come to a verdict. We find that you have wantonly engaged in conspiracy to abuse the laws of this state by using them to attack its innocent and most honorable citizens, causing them misery, pain, and even death. You have poisoned the well of justice in Montana and it must be cleansed. Our whole economy has suffered because of you and the gang of criminals you control. You have been found guilty of the crime of treachery and it is the sentence of this court that you be hanged by the neck until you are dead."

Smith let out a loud, muffled gasp of shock. His body shuddered, his knees buckled, and he was supported upright only by the two men standing beside him. A dark blue stain appeared on the forefront of his tattered denim jeans and worked its way to his ankles as his bladder involuntarily released itself. It was all Reamy Nelson could do to control the same reactions he felt as the verdict was announced. The sentence seemed to hit Nelson like a fist in the middle of his chest, and he hoped no one heard the grunt as his breath was suddenly expelled. A board creaked beneath his feet as he fought to hold on to his composure.

The chairman went on, "You are to be hanged in a manner prescribed by the laws of this state on a gallows officially approved for the purpose. Gentlemen, take him over to the mill shed and Montana's 'Galloping Gallows' where we will carry out the execution. Mr. Smith, you are about to see your last glorious sunrise in Montana and may God have mercy on your wretched, stinking hide."

Main lift, Snowshoe, Montana

Smith was carried stumbling northward down the street to a great, black hulk of the abandoned mine milling house and into the darkened interior. The approaching sunrise cast opaque, hazy shadows about the room and echoes resounded from each footstep on the coarsely graveled floor. The group of men stood silently as Johnson joined them. "Bill, take this key and open that padlock on the manhole cover under the lift." He gestured toward the nearby mine hoist tower as he moved to the side of Reamy, Evans, and the prisoner.

A short stairway leading upward to a high platform faced them. The walkway had handrails around three sides and an erect beam was centered on its near side. From a braced horizontal beam at its top, a stiff, new, one-inch manila rope was draped to the floor and upward to the railing. It was formed into an oblong slipknot loop that was secured by thirteen wraps of rope. From below, one could make out the shape of a square trapdoor in the center of the platform, mounted with two large hinges on one side. The trapdoor was held closed by a pivoting wooden board with its end fitted into a rectangular iron bracket. A smaller rope was attached to the opposite end of the board which was carried through a pulley and strung upward to the railing at the top of the stairs.

Smith looked upon the structure briefly, only to let his mind realize that this device was soon to be the last earthly thing in his vision. His chin dropped to his chest as shuddering sobs surged through his body. "Evans, I'll help you take him up the stairs," said Johnson. "It's my job to fix the noose and pull the latch. They lurched forward, dragging Smith upward between them to the center of the trapdoor. As Johnson took the noose in hand, he went on, "Take his belt off and bind him around the ankles with it, Walt."

The noose was cinched around Smith's throat as he stood facing to the East. Johnson balanced the heavy knot on his right shoulder and spoke again, "That's good, Walt. You can go back down with the others now."

Smith heard footsteps descending the stairs and looked up through the high openings under the millhouse roof to see the bright pink of morning sky merge with the silky topaz of a new day. He heard the sudden rasp of wood grating against wood and, for an instant, he became weightless. Then there was blackness and silence.

The trapdoor clattered as Smith instantly plummeted into the empty space in front of the onlookers. His spasms lasted less than a minute because the heavy knot positioned between his jaw and ear had broken his neck quickly and mercifully. All was silent except for the hollow, groaning sounds of the gallows, then the interruption of Johnson's footsteps on the platform that echoed throughout the millhouse.

"Bill, bring that stretcher over from the corner there. Boys, I'll cut him down and you be prepared to lay him out on the stretcher."

When the deceased Smith and the remains of his new rope were in position, three men on each side of the stretcher hoisted him to arm's length and turned to follow Johnson out of the millhouse and along a path for some 20 yards toward a wide concrete slab. In its center was a black hole 28 inches in diameter, and beside it laid the manhole cover and an opened padlock. This was the top of the old mine's largest vertical shaft.

Above the slab stood the massive beams of the main hoist used to carry men and materials in an out of the tunnels far below before mining operations had ceased some 60 years before. "Aim him right down that hole, boys. Let him fly down and join the others waiting for him."

With that done, the steel cover was replaced and locked over its position on the concrete slab. Johnson folded the stretcher and began to carry it back to the millhouse. As he faced the group of motionless men, he said, "It's a difficult, but fair piece of justice we have carried out here, gentlemen. You are a tribute to the Brigade and the finest kind of people Montana could produce to undertake the ugly kind of work that comes with preserving the foundations of our beloved state. Thank you all! You can get on back to your places now. I will take care of the small details around here."

Nelson was still stunned and oblivious to his surroundings as he hurried to his parked Blazer and somehow got it into motion down the narrow winding pathway that led out of Snowshoe. The vision of the chilling scene he had witnessed would replay in his mind throughout the two-and-a-half hour drive from there to Bigfork, over and over again, while painful surges of terror, guilt and remorse invaded his senses. He felt that he too had fallen into a deep chasm of darkness as surely as had Arleigh Smith.

Reamy Nelson was a third-generation Montanan, native son of Bigfork and an eight-year veteran as a constable with the Bigfork police. He had a charming wife and six-year-old daughter. Nelson was one of the most devoted and reliable officers ever to serve the community and, in his sixth year, was inducted into the Justice Brigade as one of its youngest members.

To the young officer, receiving such an honor was equal to becoming an Eagle Scout or receiving the Medal of Honor. By becoming one of the Brigade, he had achieved a hallowed place in life that paid homage to rugged vigilantes that loomed larger than life in the stories he had absorbed from his ancestors since early childhood. Nelson truly believed that the Justice Brigade was a social order established to memorialize the vigilantes and honor the best of modern Montana law enforcement. It had never occurred to him that the organization might be carrying out serious vigilante activities, as this certainly was, in present times.

Nelson arrived in Bigfork early in the afternoon, having eaten nothing on the way. His appetite had been replaced with a tension in his stomach that allowed no room for food. The afternoon was occupied contemplating his situation at a favorite secluded place on a ridge facing the upper bays of Flathead Lake. Reamy remained there long after sunset and, while slowly making his way home, realized that he had been unable to reach any conclusions that could penetrate the dark clouds of his anxieties.

After a sleepless night, he resumed his customary Saturday schedule, beginning with breakfast in the company of fellow Brigade members, Burton Davis of the Montana Highway Patrol and Jerry Ackerman, a sergeant with the U.S. Border Patrol. When they were seated and their usual orders placed, Reamy said, "Well, guys, I finally did some committee work for the Brigade Thursday night. It's been a long week."

"So, you were on a committee?", asked Ackerman. "I don't suppose you wound up banishing anyone, huh?", he chuckled.

"Nope, it wasn't like simply handing him a paper with '3-7-77' on it—much worse. This is the first time I have been invited to sit on a committee, and they gave me the job of being a defense counsel. I worked like hell to get prepared and had only a couple of hours to do it. I'm ashamed to say that I never thought it might be a vigilante committee. Hell, I figured they went away years ago! Burt, when you and I worked on that Jeep Rogers snatch, that was the only Brigade work I was ever asked to do. It seemed more like a prank than anything else. I didn't consider that job really harmful, but I still don't know what ever happened to him. Possibly he wound up serving a life sentence someplace, but surely not in Montana."

"Well," said Davis, "we don't usually talk about the accused or the nature of cases among ourselves, so I won't ask about the details of your committee work. Main thing is that someone thought enough of you to bring you into a committee and I know you did your best. Welcome to the club! However . . . since you brought up the Rogers' thing . . . yes, he was sentenced to life and he is serving it out somewhere in Montana.

"Now I suppose your committee could have resolved something a little more serious than the Rogers' case. If so, that would be on the order of a hanging verdict, and if you didn't expect that to happen, I guess you believed very strongly in the defense you made for the guy. Anyhow, you were called and did your duty best as you could. I don't think the Brigade has a big backlog of work to do, so you may not be called again. Even so, you don't have to accept any committee work and no one gets upset if you turn it down."

For Nelson, there was no encouragement or satisfaction to be gained from the conversation with his two friends. They finished breakfast and went to their separate assignments. Through his shift, Nelson was unable to focus his thoughts on anything other than the tremendous mental burden he carried. His conscience needed a haven, and he thought deeply about where that might be.

He felt that he had conspired with no one to become involved in the death sentence that was carried out at Snowshoe the day before. He had done all he could to defend Smith and truly felt that his opinions would have some weight on the case. They didn't. He was not guilty of conspiracy or murder, and he worked out the details in his mind to clear himself of it all. Seeking a way out of his dilemma must be done with utmost care and absolute secrecy.

When he arrived at home after work, he explained to his wife that he needed to be left alone and not be disturbed in order to complete some very serious computer documentation work. Armed with a light snack and a carafe of hot coffee, he opened a web search for name and address information required for his letter. Soon, he entered the date on an open word processor image and began typing:

EXTREMELY SENSITIVE AND CONFIDENTIAL

Mr. Harold Clay
Attorney General of the United States
Department of Justice Office Building
Washington, D.C.

Dear Mr. Attorney General:

You are the only conceivable source I can turn to as I struggle with the most serious difficulty I have ever faced. I trust you to help me, knowing that my life is at risk by communicating with anyone in this manner.

I am a constable with the Bigfork police department and a member of a professional "elite" of Montana law enforcement known as the Justice Brigade. Yesterday, I participated on a committee of Brigade members who held a quasi-court session to hear the case of a man accused of "treachery."

I was selected to defend him and, although I did my level best to make a case for his innocence, he was found guilty and sentenced to hang! The hanging and disposal of his body was done in my presence and there was nothing I could do to prevent it.

I have no way of determining the numbers of vigilante cases handled in this way or how many people may be involved. The Justice Brigade has no roster of members that I know of and its leadership is unknown. I have heard that Brigade members serve in almost every area of law enforcement in the state, our judiciary, and even in our government, but have no way of proving any of that.

It is my deepest concern that the single case in which I have found myself unwittingly involved warrants the most serious action possible to eradicate the kind of horrible criminal conspiracy I have witnessed.

I am, therefore, appealing to you to fully investigate my concerns and have the matter brought before a federal grand jury as soon as possible. I may be the only source of information ever to come forward in this way, and I trust that some form of immunity may be granted to me for my willing participation in the investigation and prosecution of Justice Brigade members.

There is the gravest personal risk in bringing this matter to you, and I hope you will urgently respond.

Sincerely,

Nelson included his personal address and phone number, and signed the letter for mailing at the post office the next day.

Four days later, he received a call from an assistant attorney general in Washington, D.C., in which an appointment was made the following week for him to interview in the Bigfork area with two special investigators. They arrived in a special, unmarked, executive jet aircraft at Kalispell International Airport and discreetly met with Nelson over three consecutive nights at a Columbia Falls motel.

His debriefing was extremely difficult. The men wanted verifiable facts, leads to other witnesses and items of physical evidence. All he was able to provide were his Justice Brigade ring, the secret 800 number and the fact that Arleigh Smith had, by now, been officially listed as a missing person. He also briefed them on his participation in the kidnapping of athletic celebrity, Jeep Rogers, and the rumor that he was unlawfully incarcerated somewhere in Montana.

He was relieved to get official assurances of immunity from prosecution and very gratified over the manner in which the investigators handled the case. The two men departed to make use of an undetermined time to establish some groundwork on the case, alerting Nelson to be "on-call" for subsequent meetings. Three agonizing days passed before he heard from them again. They would meet in a different motel in Kalispell and Nelson was warned to be particularly cautious he wasn't being followed.

One of the agents began, "Well, Reamy, we checked a few things out about as far as we could go without jeopardizing you and came up with some real dead-ends.

"First, the '800' number you gave us is listed to a florist in San Jose, California. We are having him checked out."

The other agent spoke, "We hung around a number of areas frequented by cops between here and Missoula and saw no one wearing that little 'JB' ring. In casual conversation with one cop, he said he had heard about the Justice Brigade and that it was only some kind of honor awarded to men and women who do a good job. The guy we talked to had no idea we were feds, so you can relax about that."

The first agent again spoke, "Now, the big problem. This Arleigh Smith person, yes, he came up missing on the day you said. But get this, he was stopped by a highway patrolman and given a ticket about 20 miles from where his car was left on the Blackfoot Highway at a fishing access site. The next day, another patrolman on that same beat thought the car had been parked too long there and became suspicious. He found a copy of the signed traffic ticket in the car and a baggie of pot hidden in the passenger seat. They confirmed the owner's registration, his address in Missoula, and checked out a couple of communes where he was supposed to be. Smith could not be located, so they began a manhunt.

"Three days later, according to Missoula authorities, Smith's badly decomposed and animal-ravaged body was found down the Blackfoot about 5 miles from his car. Only scraps of his clothing and a few personal effects remained. His watch, ring and wallet were given to his female playmates, and he was buried in the Missoula Cemetery yesterday."

The other agent spoke, "As to what you said about Jeep Rogers, all we can confirm is that he was reported missing in Montana and is still listed as such, presumed dead. We have no leads other than you to proceed with. We took a helicopter tour out to Snowshoe and found it like you described. There is a rugged little trail leading in, and it's a dead-end. No way could we safely inspect it as a crime scene without someone becoming aware. That's private property out there and we would need a warrant."

Reamy could hardly believe his ears. The few pieces of information he was able to offer could give no support for his story. "Obviously, guys, that '800' number is answered by someone connected to the JB. It doesn't make sense that only a florist in California uses it. You are bound to find a link there. As to the ring, I know you weren't able to get into the information about the organization without alerting someone. I can understand that. But the body of Arleigh Smith buried? No! It couldn't be him. It had to be some other corpse they got somewhere, or maybe they faked everything out and just buried a bundle of rocks and sand, road kill . . . . whatever."

The first agent continued, "We are unable to confirm anything you gave us, but that isn't important at this point. Your complaint still stands with the Department and will simply require lots more work. We can't go for a warrant on Snowshoe or go to court to exhume the remains of Arleigh Smith, yet. We are at a wall until we have something more to go on."

"Yes," said Reamy, "it may take a long time. But, I'm worried! If word got out that I snitched about the hanging, then I'm a dead man! Seems like they have covered up everything very carefully though . . . even you all can't come up with any leads."

The second man spoke again, "Every conceivable precaution has been taken to protect you, Reamy. We report directly to the attorney general and no one else. All of our communications go only to him, as with our initial report from here. He will want to broaden the investigation into the whole of the JB organization and not just the case you reported. Someone else will come to us with a piece or two and it will be enough for a grand jury. When that happens, you will be in the clear completely. Meanwhile, we have only you and your story."

"Yes," added the first, "you maintain a very low profile and keep everything to yourself. You will be hearing from us in a couple of weeks. You should be okay."

With that, he took leave of them in the motel. There was no turning back. It was now all up to them.

CHAPTER 16

The Fish Trap

One of mankind's earliest, most successful engineering accomplishments has been the invention of stream fish traps. The devices, found in all early cultures, were fashioned from reeds, tree roots, strips of bark, willows, bamboo or small tree branches. A fish trap generally resembled a large, cylindrical basket, with one end closed. The opposite end had an open, cone-shaped structure fashioned into the container for the purpose of funneling fish from the wide mouth into a small opening at the apex. The ribs which made up the trap walls were spaced so that the largest of the intended fish species could enter and the smallest fish escape.

The combined device was weighted to remain on a stream bottom and the mouth of the cone was placed downstream to allow the fish, following their normal movements upstream, to be channeled into the trap. Once fish found their way into the larger chamber, they were unable to retrace their route into it and would become imprisoned until the trap was removed from the stream.

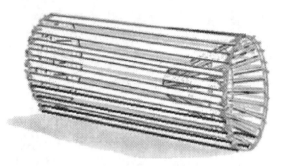

Stream fish trap

So it is, that the peculiar geography of the West has naturally formed "fish traps" to subtly guide visitors from the southwestern states into vast, beautiful Montana. While being channeled northward by the outstretched fingers of the Rocky Mountains on U.S. 93, Interstate 15 or Interstate 90, the traveler is guided imperceptibly by natural features into the restricted notches of mountain passes which ultimately open into the wide frontiers of the state.

One of the most traveled of "fish trap" journeys from the South into Montana is the route of Interstate 25. As the highway enters the mouth of the great barren triangle of Wyoming plains north of Colorado, it becomes bounded on the west by the Laramie Mountains, and on the east, by rugged, trackless badlands.

As one proceeds northward toward the intersection of Interstate 25 and Interstate 90 near Buffalo, Wyoming, the westward walls of the funnel grow gradually closer as the Bighorn Mountains come into view. From there, the traveler crosses through high, rolling hills at the narrow end of the funnel on Interstate 90 to enter Montana and the reservation of the Crow Indian Nation. There, the terrain offers very limited options of travel, other than the Interstate route and, if the visitor happens to be a "big fish" fugitive of justice, he has unwittingly entered a natural capture chamber with little chance of escape. Over the years, a number of fugitives have made such a mistake.

Sergeant Charles Runner, a native citizen of the Crow Nation, was a central figure of the Crow tribal police force for 17 years. He served two enlistments with the U.S. Army Special Forces as a sniper, with multiple combat assignments, and is an 8-year veteran of the Montana Justice Brigade.

The Runner family has been closely affiliated with national military service through all of America's wars, dating back to Corporal Ignace Runner, a scout for General George A. Custer and the 7th U.S. Cavalry Regiment. No one could be more suited to the assignment he occupied in the tribal police force. Runner is the intrepid individual who excels at working alone and knows almost every rugged square foot of the Crow Nation. For those reasons, he never accepted multiple opportunities to serve as chief of police in the Crow Nation government.

Over the years, Runner devoted his expertise to monitoring the "fish trap" where the Crow Nation bounds Interstate

90. His success numbered in the hundreds of fugitives captured single-handedly, winning him the praise of law enforcement officials from many states and agencies of the federal government.

At the morning briefing before beginning his shift, the entire tribal police force was assembled on a matter of extreme urgency. They were being enlisted to join other law enforcement officials in Montana in an all-points alert for three suspects who had broken out of Meador County jail in Franklinville, Texas, the previous day. Two of the fugitives were convicted of murdering a service station attendant and three patrons in Franklinville and were awaiting transportation to death row at Huntsville State Penitentiary. The third was originally from Montana and grew up in the Miles City area. He had been arrested in nearby Bowie, Texas, for the murder of the family he was living with while working as a farm hand. Both parents and three young children died from multiple knife wounds.

The escapees had stolen a guard's private vehicle and firearms, and were suspected to be traveling northward, possibly to Montana. Although the guard's vehicle had not been found, authorities presumed the fugitives might have changed vehicles and managed to flee the state of Texas. Traveling cautiously, they could be in northern Nebraska, Colorado, or even Wyoming by the time Crow police were notified.

The Crow police chief placed off-duty patrols on stand-by status and assigned the remainder of the shift to watching various sectors on the reservation paralleling each off-ramp from Interstate 90. All were given these specific instructions, except Sergeant Runner. The chief knew this task was something he could handle on his own discretion.

When the briefing finished, Runner left hurriedly in his cruiser to pick up bottled water and snacks at Crow Agency for an extended tour of his favorite observation points in the foothills of the Bighorn Mountains. As he parked in front of the Conoco Quick Stop, his radio crackled with a message from his dispatcher. "Charlie, we just got a phone call asking you to get in touch with '3-7-77,' whatever that means."

"Ten-four, Charlotte-Jan. I know what that means. Thanks."

Runner made his way from the cruiser to the outside pay phone at the station and dialed the memorized "800" number that was answered by an anonymous deep voice, in an unknown place, beginning with "Greetings brother!" Runner identified himself to the voice which responded, "Charlie, if those three fugitives are on their way to Crow Nation, we have no doubt that you will be the one to find them. We are particularly interested in the smaller one of the two Texans. His name is Eddy Neff, and we need him for another purpose.

"If you can work it out, we would like to have you take him into custody separately under the guise of an escape, and hold him until another one of our officers can pick him up. If he resists and gets killed, that would be second best but we would still need his corpse, and without bullet holes. The other two convicts should be turned over to Billings authorities who will keep them for extradition back to Texas."

"Do you mean hold him or his dead body but report that he has escaped?" asked Runner.

"That's right," answered the voice.

"Well, with all the personnel involved out here, I think it will have to be arranged at night so that a faked escape can work. Wouldn't want too many witnesses hanging around to dispute what went on."

"That's correct. Not even the other prisoners should know what happened to Neff so take your time to get him just right. Do you think you can handle it?"

"Yeah," replied Runner. "I think I can make it look like Neff escaped, but what do I do with him afterward?"

The voice responded, "Good enough, Charlie. We have to make a couple of contacts to arrange for someone to take him off your hands. So, call back in a half hour. Is it all set with you?"

"Sure," he acknowledged, and the voice closed the conversation.

Within minutes, U.S. Border Patrolman Martin Scott at Cutbank, Montana, was in telephone contact with the "voice" that had specific instructions for him. "Greetings brother, we need your help on an urgent matter. Do you suppose you could get a day off for some extended vehicle travel? It would mean leaving with little notice."

"Sure," Scott responded. "I think I could arrange that. What can I help you with?"

The voice came back, "We would like to have you stand by to pick up a prisoner by the name of Eddy Neff from Charlie Runner at Crow Nation and transport him to some of our people over near Bigfork. He might be alive, might be dead but it's a very discreet scenario that we can't fully discuss. We need this guy for a very special purpose.

"When you have him in custody, highway patrolman, Bill Ready, in the Bigfork area, will give you specific instructions on where to deliver the guy. It will be somewhere out in the woods away from Bigfork. Just make contact with him on the police band and follow through with all other communications by telephone."

"I think I have the idea," said Scott. "Just give me a few hours lead time so that I can get off shift or arrange whatever is needed. Happy to help out."

"Thank you, Martin. You will be hearing from us soon, whether it is on or off."

The next call from the voice went to Timberline County Sheriff, Brigham Johnson.

"Greetings brother! We are getting ready for the possibility of a piece of work that may need your attention. I guess you have heard about the alert sent out on those three killers that escaped from Texas?"

"Yep. I hear they might be headed for Montana, but I am quite a ways from any place they might enter," said Johnson.

The voice continued, "No one is sure if they will wind up here or not, but in case they do, there is one of them we want for special handling. His name is Eddy Neff and he fits the description of someone who needs to be found dead in a mountain auto accident and subsequent fire.

"Neff has already been given the death penalty in Texas and the Council of Ten has held a session and condemned him to hang if he shows up here in Montana. We would like you and a couple of your associates to carry out his sentence and handle the disposition of his remains. However, it won't be quite like the Arleigh Smith matter you took care of out at Snowshoe."

"Well, no problem with our being prepared if we get our hands on them. How are you going to cover carting one of them away from the others? And, go through that part again about the disposal of his carcass, will ya?"

"He will just have a second escape. Alive or dead, we will get him to you. If he is still kicking, give him a proper hanging from the nearest stout tree limb out there in the woods near Bigfork. Someone will bring you personal effects to plant on the body and by that time you will know where the abandoned vehicle is.

"You can get his body into it along with the personal effects and roll it off over a cliff where it will crash and catch on fire. A hot fire! Another one of our guys will handle the discovery and accident investigation later. We trust you to make your part happen. Any problems as you see it?"

Johnson paused a moment in deep thought over what he had heard. It was a complicated request, but one that he could manage with the help of a couple of his friends. "Nope, I don't see any problems with all of that," he replied. "You guys will just have to do the coordination and it will all come out just fine. Of course, first we have to catch that goddamned bunch of killers, right?"

"You've got that right, Brig. A lot depends on just that, and we feel we have a good chance of doing so. We appreciate your cooperation and you will be hearing from us again about whether or not you have some work to do. Goodbye for now."

Watching the clock in the White Deer Café, Charlie Runner saw his appointed time arrive, finished his coffee and sweet roll, and stepped outside to the nearby public phone booth. He dialed the "800" number and immediately made contact with the baritone voice at the other end, "Greetings brother. Do you have something for me?"

"I'm ready here and anxious to hit the trail. I need to know who will be taking the prisoner off my hands if I catch him and how that will be handled," he said.

The voice replied, "Call here as soon as you have him in custody. Then transport him from Crow Nation on out Interstate 90 toward Bozeman. Set up a location where you can monitor a public phone booth without drawing attention and give us that number. You will be met there by a Border Patrol Officer named Martin Scott who will carry him to where he is needed. That will wind up your part in the project and you can resume your duties trying to locate the "escapee" out on the rez. Will you be able to cover any accountability problems with your department?"

"I'm okay on that, for sure," chuckled Runner. "Hell, most of the time they don't know where I am, anyhow! That's a pretty fair piece of work you have laid out here for me, but no problems. Some day we will have to have coffee and get more acquainted."

"How do you know we haven't met already?" answered the voice, as he ended the conversation in a humorous tone.

Without delay, Runner mounted his Land Cruiser and set off on one of the many unimproved dirt roads that brought him into the high crags of the Bighorn Mountains. He traveled cross-country in 4-wheel drive for the final mile to reach the northern side of a precipice where he could observe all of the southward terrain as far as Wyoming. He concealed the vehicle in a thicket of juniper trees and unpacked his equipment.

A warm breeze and fresh scented air surrounded him in the brilliant midday Montana sunshine as he positioned a folding chair, shooting bench, binoculars and spotting scope between two rock ledges on the high ridge line. An assortment of bottled water, commercial beef jerky and canned fruits made up his preparations for an extended stay at his viewing platform. He had been here many times before and was trained both in the military and in his native background to be comfortable in such surroundings for many days and nights, if necessary.

Several years prior, he had found a Russian army night telescope for sale in a military surplus catalog and purchased it from his own resources. It was expensive at $1,100, but well worth the investment in the kind of work he enjoyed. Charles Runner was a professional man-hunter and proud of it.

He relaxed in his chair and began intently scanning the panorama below him, from the fringes of the far distant Wind River Mountains, to the Pryor Mountains and lower foothills of the Bighorns. Any telltale wisp of dust that came into view could reveal a vehicle traveling cross-country or along any one of the hundreds of small vehicle tracks that crisscrossed the distances. Occasionally, he raised his binoculars to check out suspicious sightings, only to discover summer dust devils as they played and departed on the landscape before him.

At the time Sergeant Runner was positioning himself on the far heights to the north of them, a small party of off-road travelers was relaxing in the shade grove several miles to the west of Interstate 25. There, the three men waited for sunset with their car hidden beside a small stream that meandered through steep clay ravines on its way out of a far canyon in the Wind River Mountains of Wyoming. Their journey had taken them from northern Texas, across the panhandle of Oklahoma and through eastern Colorado into Wyoming. By way of country roads that generally paralleled Interstate 25, they had traveled by night in a maroon Buick stolen two days previously from a very large used car lot in Lawton, Oklahoma.

The trio was fortunate that their escape vehicle was not found and the car theft had not yet been discovered. They were prison escapees from Franklinville jail in Texas and they all had murder charges or convictions weighing on their shoulders. The group was lightly armed, desperate, extremely wary, and determined to find freedom and anonymity in the wide, uninhabited reaches of Montana where the youngest of the three was taking them.

At a small filling station in Kit Carson, Colorado, the three had bartered the spare tire and wheel from their first stolen vehicle for a tank of gasoline in the Buick and several dollars worth of snacks. By the time they reached their present location, they were running short of both. "Neff," said one of the men, "we're going to have to get gas and something to eat soon, and you say we are going to need another vehicle?"

"Yes, we are," replied Neff. "There is no way we can get into Montana on the Interstate, but I know all the back trails and open prairie leading from here to there. We can't handle that terrain in this Buick. We have to get our hands on a four-wheel-drive rig and we will be okay. I think it will be easy to find one at some of the ranches around here, but we had better start scouting things before dark."

"Uh, okay, but we better get some food, too," said another. "Damned little to eat since jail two days ago, and I am getting hungry and mean about it!"

With that, the trio returned to the Buick that was soon trailing a low plume of dust as they drove slowly northward onto the Wind River Indian Reservation. Within a half hour they passed a green Isuzu Trooper coming toward them which turned onto a farm lane a few hundred yards to the rear. They turned around to follow.

The green Trooper came to a stop beside a small cottage surrounded by several aging outbuildings and abandoned vehicles. The fugitives waited at a distance until they saw the young man leave the Trooper and enter the rear of the house, then slowly eased the Buick down the lane and pulled in close behind it. It was the home of Tom Early Bear, his wife, and 12-year old daughter.

On the following morning, after Early Bear failed to show up for work, his supervisor at the Tribal Road Department came to inquire at the home. He discovered that Early Bear and his family had been brutally murdered. The tribal police were summoned who, in turn, informed the FBI in Laramie. The gruesome crime scene revealed that Tom had been shot at close range, just inside the door, and the wife and daughter raped and stabbed to death. Their green Trooper, hunting weapons and ammunition known to be owned by Early Bear were missing. A Buick bearing Oklahoma plates was parked in the back yard. The FBI added information to the fugitive alert that the three escapees from Texas were prime suspects in the Wyoming murders and were fleeing in a green Isuzu Trooper.

The sun began to set behind the mountains, stretching shadows of ever lengthening blurs in shades of purple and maroon across the prairie. The broadcasted alert had come to Sergeant Runner as his attention became focused on a slender trail of dust approaching from the south. It was too far distant for him to determine its description, even with binoculars, but it was definitely a vehicle out of place in such a deserted region. He decided that he had enough time to make a concealed approach to intercept the unidentified traveler at a place of his choosing, in a dry wash far below his outpost. He quickly gathered and loaded his equipment and supplies into the Land Cruiser, and set off slowly over the barren ridges to the rear of his observation position.

As quiet darkness began to invade the gentle canyons and pastures of the open range, Runner guided his vehicle into them, moving unseen, but steadily, into the path that he knew his quarry would be taking. At a place where the unused roadway declined steeply to make the crossing of a dry streambed, he concealed the Land Cruiser in a thicket of poplar and willows, removed his shortened police 12-guage shotgun and filled its magazine with five size '00 buckshot' loads. Then he crept into the underbrush a few yards away where he could stand hidden within three feet of the road's track.

Runner's plan was to allow the vehicle to approach close enough to recognize anyone inside. If it was the escapees, he could use two shotgun blasts to flatten the front tires and prevent the vehicle from getting out of the dry wash. From concealment, he could easily force a capture or engage in combat strictly on his terms because there would be no way back out of the streambed except through him.

The officer would wait more than an hour until the moving glow of headlights illuminated the ridgeline above him. Then the lights came into full view as the vehicle swung toward him and crept down into the gully where he waited. He recognized the pickup truck and soon identified the occupants. It was driven by a distant relative, Pious Tom. As it passed slowly within his reach, Runner clearly saw Tom seated with his young nephew beside him. As evidenced by the freshly dressed antelope in the truck bed, they had been south into Wyoming and had a successful hunt.

He saw them, but they had no idea that another human being was anywhere around. Runner had lost the advantage of his prime viewing position to check out a false lead. Now he had to quickly return to the outpost without the use of his headlights to resume the watch for his quarry. Excellent night vision, clear skies and a rising three-quarter moon allowed him to easily traverse the open range areas, and he took the precaution of disconnecting his taillight wires so that he could use his brakes without being seen.

The direction he chose was generally to the northwest, behind the low ridges that faced to the south. Occasionally, he would come to the front of the terrain to pause and check out the distances below him for telltale headlights. Within an hour, he found an acceptable observation point from which he could observe the darkened valleys and dimly lit ridges from inside his vehicle. He taped his door's pressure switch closed to make sure the interior lights would not come on when it was opened.

Runner was comforted by night sounds that surrounded him: the wails of coyotes far and near, the chirps of crickets and the deep droning of bullbat nighthawks. It was his element, a primal element that touched both his aboriginal senses and the modern mechanisms that had become instinctive to him in the military: "He who owns the night owns the battlefield." He knew that the night was his, and he spent long hours in position, using the darkness to his advantage.

Sergeant Runner waited. Then far out on the prairie before him, as if by magic, there suddenly appeared a distant, shaking glint of auto headlights, so far away that it appeared as a single glowing spot. It was almost 2:45 in the morning, a time when no hunters or ranchers, certainly no tourists, would be traversing such remote terrain. Surely it was his quarry. His excitement mounted as a rush of adrenaline surged through him.

Runner fumbled to find his night flashlight with the red lens. Turning its unfamiliar glow into the rear of the Cruiser, he withdrew the encased Russian light-intensifying telescope and dismounted from the vehicle. Placing a light woolen blanket over the hood of the car, he carefully set up the scope and aimed it in the direction of the barely perceptible source of the lights far away. As he squinted through the device, focusing it for distance, the terrain below came sharply into view in subtle shades of green and pale yellow. He could now see the vehicle clearly, and both headlights became painfully bright as the energy from them was transformed into white-yellow inside the telescope.

The vehicle was approaching his direction from about 10 miles away, having just skirted the low foothills of a ridge to his right. It would pass across a relatively flat stretch of prairie before encountering the slopes of another ridge that branched out toward Runner's left. Runner was situated at the apex of a great sprawling triangle and his quarry was about to enter its base.

His best option for making the capture and a fake a prisoner escape would be within close quarters, and he needed concealment for his approach. About midway in the twisting valley below him, an old abandoned ranch occupied an early-day tribal grazing allotment. It had several standing buildings, part of a corral, and a large stand of quaking aspens where a spring once flowed, uphill from the dwellings. The stand of trees would cover his approach nicely and the buildings would provide a daytime hiding place for the fugitives, if they should find their way to it. Runner knew he could "assist" them in making such a discovery. "This cone-shaped valley is set up just like a fish trap," he mumbled to himself. "All they need is some subtle guidance into the place I have chosen for them, just like fish to a trap."

With that, the policeman secured his telescope and blanket, started the engine of the Cruiser, and slowly eased his vehicle through the sagebrush onto the reverse of the slope along a ridge sloping to his left. After a couple of hundred yards, he drove through a gentle gap and came around to the front of the ridge within view of the car below. There, he turned on his headlights and passed around a small knoll. He slowly circled to the rear of the slope and turned his headlights off. Surely, he would be seen below and that should alter some of the plans of the "visitors."

Eddy Neff was at the wheel of the Trooper as it negotiated the rutted lane that crossed the barren flats.

"What's that up there?" shouted the one in the rear seat.

"Where?" Neff shot back, startled.

"Up on that ridge! See? It's someone driving around up there at this damned hour. Ain't right!"

Neff spied the vehicle's lights before they went out of sight. "Can't figure that one. No one would be out checking cattle or poaching game at this time of morning. Hell, it's just after 3:00 a.m.!"

The passenger beside him stirred awake as the Trooper slowed to a stop. Neff extinguished the headlights as they paused to discuss the situation. "What's going on, boys? We in a rut or something?"

"No," said Neff, "we just spotted a vehicle high up that right-hand ridge there. It went out of sight, but it sure seems odd that anyone but us would be driving around at this hour. He seemed to be headed downhill, which would bring him around behind that rise and on course with where we are going. I don't think we should continue that direction."

"What do you mean?" said the one in the back seat. "Do you mean turn around and go back? No way! Soon as they discover those dead Injuns back there, we will have double the manhunt on our backs! Get us the hell out of this mess!"

The man in the front passenger seat paused and replied, "Look, boys, I'm close to the country I know best. I'll get us through all right; don't worry. Nope, we're not going back in that direction, for sure! I think we should head upward toward the rear of that guy and we will still be headed in the general direction we want. Just kind of a detour, that's all. Besides, we are going to need a place to lay up during the day, and maybe we will find a bunch of trees up there or something. Going to be daylight in a couple of more hours."

Neff spoke again. "I go for that idea, but this really has me scared. Damn! Come this far and run into the law out here in the middle of nowhere! Who else would that be? I think we should double back until we can find another big canyon to scout out and stay out of this valley here. No more lights on, either. If that's a cop, we can ditch him in the dark, right?"

"Well," said the man beside him, "We have plenty of moonlight. Keep the lights off and we will take a wide swing around to the way we came, cross-country. I can't figure who that could be either, other than the law. They will be looking around everywhere. We should be in Montana by now, so I think it will be just a few more miles until I am in more familiar country. We will try to get up into the next little valley."

Runner stopped on the ridge to watch the distant vehicle and their response. He knew he had been seen. The suspect vehicle halted with the headlights extinguished. Those were not the actions of someone innocently taking in the stars and prairie scenery in the middle of the night. It confirmed for him that he had found the escapees. Now, he must steer them into the right place.

Using the night telescope, he saw the far vehicle moving and turning slowly away from his direction. As it began to double back on its original course, Runner got his Cruiser in motion, crossing through the upper level of the draw and onto the opposite ridge. He circled to the rear and then out to face the vehicle below, turning his headlights on again. He drove exposed for about 50 yards and crossed to the rear of the ridge. When he was out of view, he again turned his lights off and slowly continued to a place where he could survey his quarry with the night scope.

"Hold on, Neff!", shouted the man in the back seat. The driver stopped the vehicle as the man continued. "I just saw another set of headlights out there on the ridge to the right! Did you see that?"

"Yes, I saw," said Neff. "Maybe it's one guy driving around lost on the high hills or whatever. Can't figure, but I know he just headed down into the upper part of the basin we were heading for, so I don't want to go there, either. If it's two vehicles scouting out the upper end of this little valley we're in, then it looks like they are done. I think they spread out on two different directions to get down to the flats. Maybe we should go on out there between them. What do you guys think?"

"I think we should stay clear of where those headlights were headed and going out here is our only choice," said the one beside him. "Hell, if one of them spotted us earlier, they aren't in any hurry to catch up to us. That doesn't act like cops, so maybe it's just some cowboys heading home from a long trip way out in the back country. Maybe hunting deer or elk at night."

The one in back grumbled, "Okay by me, but two cars prowling around like this seems pretty damned spooky! Yep. We need a place to hole up before daylight, so let's go up this here wide glen until we find some cover. I want to warm up something to eat, anyhow. If they're huntin' us, seems pretty smart for us to sneak back to where they've already looked, right?"

"Okay, here we go," replied Neff, as he turned the vehicle toward the darkened maw of the valley.

Runner watched it all from on high. They had come around and were headed up the gentle canyon toward him. He replaced the night telescope in its case and set the Cruiser in motion downhill. It would take them 20 minutes or more to find the shelter of the old ranch house and grove of trees. He would be there waiting for them.

Runner slowly crossed the upper edges of the quaking aspens and brought his vehicle within 30 feet of one of the weathered outbuildings before coming to a stop. Under the glow of the red lens of his flashlight, he inventoried the equipment he would carry. From his nylon zipper bag he withdrew a length of nylon rope, several vinyl wrist restraints, a cloth towel, a handful of 12-guage ammunition and his Tigersharp sheath knife. After packing the items into the utility pockets of his uniform, he re-checked his Glock 9mm pistol and 12-guage shotgun. Dismounting from the Cruiser, Runner draped a woolen blanket over its hood so that there could be no reflections from its headlights. He then went to the rear of the vehicle and cleared the cargo bed, reconnected the taillight wires and returned to the driver's side, leaving the rear door open.

The red-lensed penlight was exchanged for a powerful 6-cell Maglight and he carefully made his way through the rubble of the aged buildings to enter a corner where he could not be noticed. Making sure that nothing would obstruct his view down the valley toward the oncoming car, he relaxed to wait.

The wakening dawn had begun to cast pale yellow into the skies to the east, highlighting the tops of distant mountains. In the darkened valley floor, he could barely make out a growing plume of dust, softly thrusting in his direction. It was the suspect vehicle, crossing overland without headlights. His excitement grew. It would be only a matter of minutes, now.

"Guys, I have no idea where we are, at all!" said Neff.

"Well," said the passenger to his right," I know the country around here fairly well. We're on the Crow Indian Reservation and that's the east over there where it's getting light. That means we are heading mostly northwest and uphill into the Bighorn Mountains. Not much goes on out here and the few cops are just deadbeat Injun police,"

Neff interrupted, "What is that dark patch way up there in this gulch? Is that trees or what is it? Rocks?"

"Yep, it looks like a clump of trees. They stand out from everything else in the moonlight. I think that may be the place we need right now."

The green Trooper moved steadily over the terrain, growing closer to the abandoned ranch. When they were within 200 yards, they could visually make out the darkened hulks of abandoned farm buildings. The sight of them brought cheer to the three travelers and the driver urged the vehicle more quickly toward the standing remains of a large barn. He maneuvered the vehicle inside and turned off the ignition. They were now within 20 feet of where Sergeant Runner lurked in the shadows.

Neff let out a gasp of relief. "What a find this is! No one can spot us from the air and I bet there isn't a soul within 20 miles of this place. Hell, with food and water, we could hang out here for weeks! So now you guys just get your feet on the ground and relax while I go find a place to take a dump."

"Good job, Eddy! But don't take a flashlight or smoke out there. Never can be sure who is scouting around or where. I'm going to get something to eat and then take a big long snooze."

Officer Runner heard every word and watched intensely as Neff fumbled out of the old barn and lurched toward the nearest of the quaking aspen trees. Neff passed from view behind the building where Runner was hiding, and Runner moved silently to catch up with him. He stalked the man mechanically, like a large black cat, matching each of Neff's footsteps with larger strides of his own. Neff paused when Runner was within one pace of him. Runner visually measured a wide hand-breadth target above the back of Neff's belt, slightly left of his spine. Thump! The point of the shotgun butt stock landed squarely over Neff's left kidney and he crumbled to his knees, unable to utter a gasp. Pain flooded through every cell in his body as he toppled onto his right side, struggling to breathe.

Runner was astride him instantly, rolling Neff to his face and jerking his arms behind him. Within seconds, he had plastic restraints tightened around Neff's wrists and the towel bound across his mouth. With the nylon rope, he tied the man's feet together and pulled them backward to where the long end of the rope could be held tightly by a slipknot around Neff's throat. If he kicked or struggled in this position, the knot would tighten and Neff would strangle himself to death. No matter to Runner. With his sheath knife, he cut away the remaining rope and silently retraced his steps toward the barn.

Through the open doorway, Runner could barely make out the two human forms sitting on the ground opposite the Trooper. "No need trying to sneak up on them in there," he thought. "I'll just be the third man coming back." Runner paused a moment to adjust his equipment and brought the Maglight quietly up beside the hand guard of the shotgun. Making sure the shotgun would not give away his profile, he boldly stepped forward through the doorway and walked over to the two sitting men. The intense beam of the Maglight caught their faces instantly, momentarily blinding them. "It's over, boys," Runner growled. "Sit tight and let me see your hands. Now!"

The two quickly complied. "Where's the third one of you bastards? Who's missing?" No one spoke. "Lissen, goddamit! I'm going to carve you up like you did those folks at Wind River, so you might as well tell me who and where your partner is!"

The one to his left sobbed, "It's Eddy, Eddy Neff. He went out to take a shit and ain't come back. He did it all. No knife stuff. Please, no knife stuff!"

"Both of you! On your faces, hands behind your backs! Now!" shouted Runner.

The two were trussed up in the same fashion as he had bound Neff. When he was certain that the men were completely immobilized, Runner went to where Neff was hidden and untied the slipknot around his neck. He rested the shotgun upright against a tree and, with a handful of hair in his left hand and a tight grip on the back of his trousers with the other, Runner lifted Neff half way upright and dragged him to the back of the Land Cruiser. Hefting him inside, he replaced the slipknot over his neck and lashed him tightly to the floor mounts. Runner then covered him with the woolen blanket, closed the cargo door and moved the Cruiser forward to where its headlights flooded over the two captives in the barn.

Runner turned his radio on and keyed the microphone, "Hello, base. This is Charlie." He had a quick answer from his dispatcher at Crow Agency, and continued, "I have two of the three suspects in custody here. I'm at the old Cross place up Mule Valley. Going to need some help out here. One got away. His name is Neff, one of the two from Texas. Get the boss online if possible."

"Ten-four, Charlie. Great work! I'll landline the boss, if he isn't listening in."

"Never mind, Celia, I have it," the chief interrupted. "What a helluva job getting those guys, Charlie! Kinda figured you would, though. Celia, get to the FBI and get them rolling. The rest of you guys online here get over to Charlie's location, pronto!"

"Thanks, boss," replied Runner. "The missing guy is on foot. I want to get up to the high country ahead of him, if he's headed for timber cover. Need to have some of you guys get these prisoners off my hands soon!"

"Roger on the FBI, chief," said Celia.

"Charlie, this is Bill. I'm only about 25 minutes from your twenty and rolling it. Hang on to those guys and I'll handle the rest."

The police chief was on again, "Charlie, this guy can hide in sagebrush as well as timber, but he can't move around as much. I'll get to the guys in Billings and arrange for dogs, a chopper, and other aircraft to start hunting at daybreak. I'll set up my command center out there. If he doesn't get to the mountains, he will soon need another vehicle and we will be watching for him."

"Good enough, Chief. I plan to patrol the fringes of the high country and will be offline a good part of the time, getting to some good lookout spots. Let me brief you all on what happened here while you are on the way. I want to get going as soon as you get here."

The rose-pink of predawn was washing into pale yellow sky as the sergeant completed his report on the radio. Soon, he was met by another tribal officer and, after a brief discussion about the capture scene and hunt for the third prisoner, Runner was in his vehicle on his way upward and out of the shallow basin. He was headed toward the north slopes of the Bighorn Mountains where he would intersect a logging road that would take him farther northward to reach Interstate 90 near Prairie Dog National Monument. From there, it would be a three-hour drive westward to Bozeman.

The Interstate 90 entrance ramp came into view before Runner approached paved road. He stopped to check on his prisoner, only to assure himself that he was not dead. His mission was to bring the man in alive and that would be the minimum of his tolerance for the cargo he carried. He removed the blanket covering the prisoner, checked to make sure he was breathing and that there was reaction in his pupils.

"Well, Neff, you wanted to escape into Montana and you did it. But you are going to wind up someplace that neither of us knows anything about. You see, you escaped again back there, and there is a big manhunt going on looking for you right now. Of course, you will never be found and that's for certain. I would like to have sole custody of you so that, for once in history, I could take my time to give back to you exactly the kind of torture you have given to others. That's my real, true concept of justice, and I pray someday to carry it out."

His impromptu speech concluded, Runner replaced the blanket over his prisoner and resumed his drive onto Interstate 90 and toward Bozeman. He took the first exit that led him to the Diamond Shamrock convenience store on the north edge of Bozeman. Calling over his right shoulder, he spoke loudly, "Lissen up, back there! I'm going to get out of this rig for a couple of minutes, but will have you in sight. I promised to deliver you alive, but that doesn't mean with your hands and feet attached. If you make one little move under that blanket, I'll take you down by the crick and be happy to butcher you up like a goddamned pig!"

The warning given, Runner parked to the side of the store, picked up the exterior pay telephone and dialed the Justice Brigade's secret "800" number. The voice answered, "Greetings, brother," after the first ring. "I'm at an all night stop-and-rob here in Bozeman, and I have the cargo you asked for," said Runner.

"Good work, Charlie. We've heard from Martin Scott and he should be somewhere near Bozeman by now. He gave us his cell phone number, so give him a call. Make the exchange and your piece of work is done. Then, you can go back to the mountains and resume the manhunt for that Neff character," the voice chuckled.

Runner was given the cell phone number and the conversation ended. He immediately made contact with Patrolman Scott.

"Mr. Runner, I'm parked off of Interstate 90 at the Cardwell exit. There's a little creek bottom here where we can make the swap without being noticed."

Ten minutes later, the two met on a graveled lane leading to the little town of Cardwell. The prisoner was unbound, allowed to relieve himself, then handcuffed at the wrists and placed into the back seat of Scott's black Chevrolet. Neff was told that there would be no conversation on the way to Bigfork, and understood that the gag would be replaced if he uttered anything. The two police officers exchanged pleasantries and left the area in unison. Returning to Interstate 90, they continued in opposite directions. For Scott and his prisoner, it would be a five-hour ride to Bigfork. The entire time, Neff uttered only one question to Officer Scott, "What's going to happen to me?"

"I only know your name, mister. I have no idea what you have done or what is going to happen to you, so just shut up and figure it out for yourself. Any more muttering out of you and I will put on a gag that will keep you quiet for sure!"

The unmarked Chevy with federal license tags continued on Interstate 90 to change course northward on Interstate 5 near Boulder. From there, they traveled through Helena and Great Falls, and onto a Montana highway that took them westward through Marias Pass and over the high mountains of the Continental Divide. From the top of the pass, it was less than an hour's drive to Bigfork, and it was there that Scott made contact by cellular phone with Sheriff Brigham Johnson.

"Martin, on your way down from the pass, you will cross five intersecting Forest Service roads before you get to my position. I am off the highway a few hundred yards on the sixth road marked, 'Fisher Creek Access'. You should be here in about an hour and your work will be done."

Scott acknowledged and continued down the twisting highway. It was a brilliant blue Montana midday that greeted Scott's vision from the top of Marias Pass. In less than 45 minutes, he was off the main highway and onto a graveled Forest Service road. Soon, he came upon a black and white Explorer parked in the shadows of high timber at the side of the track. A gold shield on the driver's door read, "Timberline County Sheriff."

Pulling to a halt behind the vehicle, he emerged to greet Sheriff Johnson. Without delay, the prisoner was in the sheriff's custody, and Scott turned his vehicle around to return to the highway. His trip was nearly over and he was relieved by the thought that he would be home by early evening, and no one would be aware of the lengthy tour of western Montana he had made this day.

Sheriff Johnson drove southward on the Forest Service road, with Neff pleading with him for answers about where they were and what fate was in store for him. "Shut up, you murdering bastard! You'll find out soon enough, and you're getting more slack than you gave that Indian family back at Wind River. Just remember that!"

After driving some 5 miles of the graveled road that snaked through high evergreen forest, Johnson brought the vehicle up a long rise to a ridge top. He left the roadway and maneuvered some 50 yards through sparse timber to where three cars were parked. Two of the vehicles had typical police markings and the third vehicle was a pickup truck with a high wooden crate in the truck bed. As they came to a halt, three men came forward to roughly remove Neff from the rear of Johnson's vehicle.

Supporting him by the arms, they took him to the pickup truck, roughly lifted him onto the cargo bed and seated Neff atop the wooden crate platform. As his ankles were being bound with his belt, Johnson spoke, "Soon as you finish, boys, we've gotta do this proper. This guy gets to know what is going to happen to him in the same way the little family back there in Wind River learned their fate when he knifed each of them to pieces, one after the other, after he raped the women."

In an official tone, he continued, "Mr. Eddy Neff, you rotten bastard! You have been tried and found guilty of butchery in the slayings of people in Texas and that little Indian family in Wind River. Your sentence is death by hanging! We're going to do that right by God now, and may the Devil have his way with your soul forevermore! You don't get any last words, so stop blubbering and whimpering up there!"

As the men closed around him in the pickup, Neff could not find the strength to stand. His sobs echoed through tall, silent timber as unseen hands forced him upright. A rope noose draped from a large Tamarack limb overhead was fitted around his neck with the heavy knot resting on his right shoulder. He could feel the slack of the suspended rope touch his knees and he heard the truck engine start. Johnson shouted, "Give it to him, Dave!" The truck jumped forward. Neff felt motion, the instant tension of the rope tightening, and then there was silence and blackness.

As the form of Neff went through its death spasms and swung slowly in the air, the three men paused and lit cigarettes. After a few minutes, Johnson spoke again,

"Well, that settles things up with our killer here, gentlemen. Dave, you back the truck up so that we can load and haul him over to the car parked there at the hairpin curve above the crick." Before they moved, Johnson produced a pint bottle of whiskey, which he passed around before taking a large draft for himself.

Neff's remains were unceremoniously dropped into the truck bed. The drive to a small passenger car parked high on a bluff above Fisher Creek was only a short distance.

The others followed in their vehicles. When they arrived, Johnson instructed, "We've gotta get him into the driver's seat here and then roll this rig over into the ravine. After it crashes down there, it will catch fire and burn him all up. I brought some gasoline so that we can be sure of that."

The men set to work splashing the interior of the driver's compartment with gasoline. When that was finished, one of the men took a lighted cigarette and carefully twisted the top of a small paper bag around it with the ember of the cigarette inside. The car bearing Neff's body was rolled silently to the edge of the graveled road, and the bag carrying the cigarette was thrown into the back seat. Slight momentum of movement carried the car across the grass of the roadside and onward over the precipice of cliffs. With crashing and rending sounds, the car toppled end over end twice before bright flames burst out of its shattered windows. In a final avalanche of metal and fire, the vehicle came to rest by the creek at the bottom of the steep canyon.

"That just about finishes our little piece of work here, guys," said Johnson, passing the bottle around again. They watched as the flames of the burning wreckage below began to subside. Suddenly a bright blast of yellow and orange erupted into the scene as the car's gas tank exploded.

"Soon as that dies down, we can leave. I want to let you all know that the chore we did here is going to be well-covered, so don't worry about anything. A game warden, one of our guys, will find this wreck in the morning. He will call another of our boys from the highway patrol to investigate and it will all be written up as an unfortunate accident. Another unknown party will bring the patrolman some personal effects in order to identify the driver. I reckon the dead man will be someone who sure as hell deserves to come up missing. Take another swig, boys, and we'll head on out of here."

CHAPTER 17

Snowshoe, Montana

On the day Montana authorities were given the alert on the Texas escapees, Bigfork Constable, Reamy Nelson, was finishing an uneventful tour of duty on the Friday day shift and looking forward to a normal, relaxing weekend with his wife and children. His radio came to life, interrupting pleasant thoughts of his family that Nelson needed to replace the dark, swirling clouds of emotion that continued to haunt his mind with visions of the events he had witnessed two weeks before at Snowshoe.

"127 this is dispatch, come back."

"127 here, base," Nelson acknowledged.

"127, we have a phone call asking you to contact 3-7-77 as soon as possible," the dispatcher advised, in her customary monotone.

"Call 3-7-77, ten-four. 127 clear."

Nelson pulled his cruiser into a parking area beside the Ace hardware store to make the call from an outside public phone. The Justice Brigade "800" number was answered immediately by the voice. "Greetings, brother Reamy! Thanks for the prompt return of my call. Hey, I don't want to interrupt anything special you might have planned for the weekend, but we would sure like to have you join some other members in a strategy and planning session over at Snowshoe. It's a very important meeting that will surely determine the future of the organization and, as one of the younger members of the Brigade, we need your ideas."

Nelson stood stunned for a moment, a shudder running through his body as ominous feelings about revisiting Snowshoe filled his thoughts. "Uh, yeah," he replied. "Um, well, I had planned a leisurely weekend with my family for a change, but maybe I could arrange it. How long are you talking about?" His thoughts raced in mental flashes. Why couldn't the federal agents have taken me away for protection? How can I avoid this trip or turn them down without casting suspicion on myself, or showing weakness? I can't falter, now! This isn't another one of their 'jobs' so what do I have to lose? Can I act calm about it all and participate?

The voice came back, "If you could drive over this evening and spend the night there, I think you could give the group your input and be home by tomorrow night. Our destiny will be the focus of the conference and your opinions can help keep us on the right track. It's important to us that you attend, Reamy."

Breathing nervously, Nelson fought to control the steadiness of his voice. "I have an appointment this afternoon to pick up a quarter of beef from the meat processor and will have to come up with an explanation for my wife to cover this deal. But I guess you can count on me being there."

"Thanks, Reamy. We're indebted to you. You need not wear your uniform or bring your own car all the way to Snowshoe, but be sure to wear your ring because you may not know the others over there. It wouldn't look right to have a big convoy of folks making a spectacle out there, so we have arranged for your friend, Burt Davis, of the Highway Patrol to pick you up and take you with him. You can leave your vehicle safely parked wherever he tells you to meet him. Is that okay?"

"Yeah, all right," he weakly responded. "I can handle it, but for sure will have to be home tomorrow night to salvage at least a day for the wife and kids."

"Thanks, Reamy," the voice said. "It's nice to be able to count on you." The conversation ended and Nelson, shaken, returned to his cruiser to complete his shift.

Within an hour, he received another call from dispatch giving him a telephone number with which he could contact Burt Davis. Returning the call from another public telephone, Reamy was reassured by Davis. "So, Reamy, the bosses want this to be as discreet as possible and I guess that is why we are kind of carpooling to the meeting. You brought up some very sincere concerns the other day at coffee and this is a chance for you to get them off your chest and into Brigade thinking. What is a good time for us to meet?"

"Well, Burt, I am not overjoyed at the prospect of going back to Snowshoe, but will go along with what is expected of me. Maybe the group will be able to relieve some of the burdens we face when we are called to work for the Brigade.

"As to when we can leave, I have to pick up some beef after work and would like to have dinner with my family. Maybe we could meet around 6:30. Where would you like me to leave my car?"

Davis responded, "Okay, Reamy, tell you what. The shortest route to Snowshoe is over Marias Pass. I can meet you east of Bigfork, a ways up Fisher Creek. Do you know where that is?"

"Sure," replied Nelson. I have fished out there since I was a little kid. Exactly where, Burt?"

Davis came back, "There's a steep hogback ridge with a hairpin turn a couple of miles off the highway where we can hide your car and it will be convenient when we return. How's that sound?"

"Sounds fine to me," said Nelson. "I'll see you there at 6:30."

Constable Nelson's shift closed without exceptions and he followed through with the plans he had arranged with

Davis. By 6:00 p.m. he was on his way to the meeting place and arrived early atop the steep ridge overlooking Fisher Creek. He parked off the road behind some alder bushes, confident that his vehicle would be safely hidden from the view of any passersby. With a good view down the road he had taken, Nelson sat down on a fallen lodge pole log to watch for the arrival of Patrolman Davis. In another 5 minutes, Davis joined him and they retraced their approach on the Forest Service road to return to the Marias Pass highway. The trip to Snowshoe would take three hours and Nelson was anxious to share more of his thoughts about the Brigade with his friend, Burton Davis.

Full darkness surrounded them before they reached the foothills east of the Continental Divide. To relax and consume time, the two travelers talked of trivial things, such as fishing spots, picnics, mountain hikes, hunting trips and family outings, even though Nelson's mind was painfully focused on the mysterious, dark side of the Justice Brigade. At an appropriate opportunity to shift the conversation to his concerns, Nelson raised an opening question, "So, Burt, did you ever hear of anyone resigning from the Justice Brigade?"

Davis paused for several seconds, contemplating his answer. "Hell, I only know of about a half-dozen officers who belong to the Brigade and you're one of them. We don't always wear our rings, anyhow," chuckled Davis. "I never thought of the Brigade as that kind of an organization, Reamy. To me, it's kind of like being on the

National Honor Society or something like that, and who would think of resigning from the NHS? Only difference is that we aren't high school kids anymore. We are in law enforcement where people depend on us to administer to the needs of justice in this state. We all know that the laws fail to do that nowadays. It's become too complicated, and there's a loophole of some kind for every kind of criminal. We get tired of picking up the failures, and there are more of them on the streets every day."

"I sure agree with that," replied Nelson. "The early vigilantes had to cope with a mess almost as bad, but there weren't as many people in their days."

Davis interrupted, "Right! We still pay tribute to their work and the Brigade is carrying out some of it even today. I wear their secret number on my Highway Patrol patch, and that keeps us all mindful about the old guys who made us a law-abiding state. The Montana vigilantes were here and left their mark. We learned all about them in Montana history and from our elders. Did you ever hear of a vigilante resigning? Hell, I never heard that they even closed shop!"

Reamy thought aloud, "They didn't close shop. We are the Montana vigilantes, but no one seems to know our size or strength. When we accept the honor represented by the ring and the induction, we take an oath of loyalty to the organization and to law and order. Nothing is mentioned about what we may be called upon to do. Maybe we should try to change that."

"Could be that can change, but I doubt it," Davis proposed. "One thing is that with honor there comes added commitment and responsibility in almost anything a person does. The second thing is that someone has to do the dirty work, and that may occasionally come our way, too. The old-timers had to chase the bad guys down, hold courts, hand out verdicts and carry out sentences of banishment or hanging. We do the same in law enforcement every day and, thankfully, never find ourselves doing every scrap of it. The vigilantes had to do it all."

Nelson was still unsettled. "You know, I thought my first assignment snatching Jeep Rogers meant banishment for him, but you surprised me when you said he was in jail somewhere. Banishment or imprisonment I can handle. However, hanging someone is what I really have problems with."

"Figure it this way, Reamy. There isn't a state hangman in Montana anymore because we have death by lethal injection. There is still a person assigned to be state executioner, and he does his job. If the Brigade hands out death penalties, I'm sure I wouldn't be asked to do every lynching and neither would you. But I would be happy to put the noose on at least one of the bastards because I know the Brigade wouldn't hand that out to anyone who didn't deserve it. I'll bet some of the old vigilantes felt the same way as you, but they stuck with it and cleaned up the territory in good shape."

Nelson drifted into silent thoughts about their discussion as they bounced slowly along the old rough mining road that took them into Snowshoe. As they entered the deserted town, the reflected taillights of several vehicles parked in front of the courthouse cast red, eye-like glances at them. Nelson shuddered. Snowshoe starkly reminded him of ultimate evil. It was as if a host of devils was glaring at them from the darkness.

They left their car, stretched, and made their way to the building with windows lighted from inside by the subtle, flickering glow of kerosene lamps. Before they entered, Reamy could smell the scent of pine smoke from the old iron stove and the sweet odor of brewed coffee. Creaking sounds measured their strides as they mounted the wooden steps before entering the vestibule of the courtroom. Reamy glanced down the opposite side of the moonlit street to the building under the black lift tower where the hanging of Arleigh Smith had taken place. He swallowed hard and struggled to keep his composure.

Inside the door, Reamy quickly counted seven people. Three men stood with their backs to him, ignoring their arrival. A quick glance assured him that some wore the little rings matching his on their right small fingers. The men parted as a slender, middle-aged woman in a long black dress stepped forward to greet him. Fumbling with a slender gold chain at her neckline, she approached to within a few paces of Reamy. "Hello, Mr. Nelson, sorry to bring you here under false pretenses."

Nelson winced, wild thoughts struck deeply into his brain. *False pretenses? Have I been set up? What can she mean, false pretenses?*

"I'm Anita Martin, U.S. Attorney for the federal district in Butte. The U.S. Attorney General has forwarded your case to me for grand jury proceedings."

"U. S. Attorney! Whew!" Nelson gasped. His confusion began to clear as new hopes flooded into his mind with a warm sense of relief that swept over the cold dampness of his limbs. He knew his call for help had been answered! Silently, he shuddered with disbelief, thinking, *They have come together here to work on my case, Brigade members and all! I am free of torment, saved! Thank Almighty God!*

Nelson felt two men from the rear of the room move quietly forward to flank him on either side. As Martin continued to speak, she slowly produced an object attached to a gold chain around her neck. It was a little gold ring with a deep blue Montana Yogo sapphire in its center. "But, we both know that isn't possible, don't we, Mr. Nelson? Tom Nash, here, will explain."

A torrent of fear splashed inside his head. *What?* He thought. *Not possible! But, she is here . . . with a ring! She is part of the federal court AND the Brigade!*

Nash began, "Reamy Nelson, you have been charged with the crime of treachery, and we have tried your case earnestly. You have betrayed our noble cause and endangered the lives of everyone committed to it. Reamy Nelson, you have been found guilty of the charge and it is the sentence of this committee that you be hanged by the neck until you are dead. We are going to relieve you now of your ring and other personal effects, you miserable goddamned snitch! Your sentence will be carried out immediately."

Nelson's legs became numb. Tears burst from his eyes and his racing pulse made wild drumbeats in his ears. For the moment, time stood still. As if in slow motion, he felt the men beside him tense and step forward in unison. There was a faint creaking sound of the wooden floorboards and the whisper of metal against leather as they drew their weapons. Barely able to move, Nelson glanced to his right and saw one of the agents who had interviewed him two weeks prior in Kalispell. From across the room, another man moved with his pistol drawn and shouted to all, "FBI! NOBODY MOVE! YOU ARE ALL UNDER ARREST!"

PART III

The Justice Brigade

CHAPTER 18

Path of the Brotherhood

FEDS BREAK UP VIGILANTE LYNCHING

U.S. District Attorney Arrested

Butte Union Miner
Tuesday, September 11, 2001

Working undercover, FBI agents foiled the attempted lynching of a Bigfork police officer by members of a secretive gang of law enforcement officers who belong to the Justice Brigade. The raid took place in the pre-dawn hours this morning in the old Timberline County Courthouse at Snowshoe, an early day mining ghost town.

Leading the raid was FBI Special Agent, Jim Holcomb, who said that seven law enforcement officials were arrested, including Anita Martin, U.S. Federal Attorney for the Butte District. The name of the lynch mob's intended victim was not given.

Holcomb said there may be evidence of other lynchings at Snowshoe with the mine shafts used to dispose of the remains. The Snowshoe area will be sealed off as a crime scene pending further investigation.

September 11, 2001, became the most shocking and devastating day in U.S. history when terrorists flew commercial aircraft into the Twin Towers in New York City. Had it not been for this event, the arrests at Snowshoe might have become the story of the year in the major media. However, as the legal process unfolded, the capture and investigation of seven members of Justice Brigade was seldom mentioned in Montana television or newspapers.

The story of the revival of early-day Montana vigilante activity found no place to compete with the captivating events that were chronicled everywhere by America's War on Terror. And so, the identities of suspects, the elements of criminal investigation, discovery, evidence, hearings and trial delays that ensued went by almost unnoticed by anyone close at hand and almost certainly obscured to anyone outside Montana. Secrecy of this kind in the judicial process was not planned, but certainly became an advantage to the accused and a great benefit to the Justice Brigade at large. All elements of the case were guided professionally and adeptly by the hand of U.S. District Judge R.J. Smith.

Officer Reamy Nelson, the intended victim of the lynching, was whisked away secretly by U.S. Marshals under the cloak of the Federal Witness Protection Program. His role in exposing the Justice Brigade dealt a severe blow to the organization's strength of secrecy, but his depositions became buried under stacks of court evidence that never reached the attention of the press. Agent Holcomb worked diligently to find a trail leading beyond the seven suspects to the greater vigilante network described by Nelson, all to no avail.

No records existed that would name the highest performing law enforcement officers of Montana who, over many years, were specially recognized by the Montana Vigilance Association (MVA) with appointments to the Justice Brigade. The memories of MVA officials had now become clouded when trying to recall exactly who those exceptional individuals really were. The ones accused of conspiracy to commit murder had nothing to say about the Justice Brigade and denied being part of any such organization. The little gold rings bearing the initials "JB" on either side of a Yogo sapphire were identifying emblems that were reportedly carried by all members, but no one could testify seeing them worn by anyone other than the suspects arrested at Snowshoe. Holcomb's investigation was unable to determine where the rings were manufactured.

The scope of the case became fixed on only the accused, but Holcomb knew there must be more to it than that. Out of Reamy Nelson's compartmentalized exposure to the Justice Brigade, other names were given, but they all denied being part of the Justice Brigade, and there was no way to prove they were. Holcomb reached out to his predecessor, Charles Gettys, to see if there were any other possible leads.

Charles and Janet Gettys were enjoying their first year of marriage, spending time together in the evenings; their marriage was a happy one. Both continued in their careers, but it seemed their Washington jobs were much less stressful. Charles really didn't expect to be "involved" much more in work with the Brigade, and Janet had tried to leave behind her concerns about the strange observations she had witnessed at the old prison.

Even though her reporting on the story won national recognition and her testimony in court provided a victory for the prosecution, she was unable to reconcile in her mind the many critical elements of the story that were never proven in court. She held to her belief that the activity was part of a greater conspiracy in law enforcement that had vigilante overtones, but before she was able to develop new information that would support her suspicions, Janet resigned from the *Horizon* and she and Charles made their move to Olympia.

Her new job with the *Olympia Register* brought her again into contact with law enforcement, but the job was routine and somewhat boring until reactions to 9-11 tumbled in on police forces all around the country. Both she and Charles were part of a mad scramble to handle the tidal wave of information, directives, and security weaknesses, strengthening our border with Canada and citizen referrals to suspects. The positioning of manpower at both the newspaper and the FBI office fell far below essential needs that mounted almost hourly.

In the midst of this maelstrom of activity, Charles Gettys received a call from agent Holcomb in Butte, Montana, reporting the arrests of members of the Justice Brigade. His query provided lengthy details on what was alleged, what was discovered, and the fact that they were unable to develop any leads into what Holcomb suspected was a statewide network of vigilantes. It was the first news Gettys had about the arrests in Montana and he gave a slight shudder of disbelief as he discussed details with Agent Holcomb.

"Charlie, I know you had an issue that came up here locally at the old prison where some people felt sure the players were part of a larger vigilante group working throughout the state. I mentioned that one of the people we bagged was your old friend, Anita Martin, but her lips are sealed along with the rest of the gang. Did you develop anything other than rumors when the state guys were working that case? We're running on a single kind of incident here, and I think there is more to it."

"Well, Jim, the prison thing seemed to evaporate into rumors when I was on the case. There was no report of anything of the kind anywhere else in Montana, and our efforts concluded with what we had for court. What's the status of Anita and the rest of the prisoners?"

Agent Holcomb replied with a chuckle, "They're doing better than most in the Silver Bow jailhouse. Seems that they get showers every day, changes of clothes, community room privileges, and even food catered in from several restaurants around here. Other prisoners are complaining about it too, and they are kept apart from them. I guess there is a thin line between heroes and criminals in Montana, as I am sure you are aware.

"The main problem I have is that my resources have pulled back off for other assignments, and I am saturated with new priorities that leave this case in the dust. I have tried to borrow investigators from Customs, Marshall Service and ATF, but they have none to spare. I hate to go to any local guys for help because of the implications. 9-11 has really done us in!

"Whatever I have to give to this case is on my own time, and I have little to spare. That's why I called to see if you could spare me a few minutes as soon as you can, whenever, to give me some ideas on where to go and what else I might dig into."

"Jim, I am as strung out as you on the 9-11 crunch, and I know this case represents a big priority to the folks in Montana, even if it never gets the attention of our headquarters. And it probably won't. I don't know how to detach myself from this mess for even a couple of hours but I will try. We may be able to get our heads together on ideas to help you, and maybe I can get over to Butte this weekend. I will make a plea to the boss and let you know for sure later today."

As soon as the conversation ended, Charles called his supervisor to make the strongest possible case for assisting the Bureau in Butte on a possible statewide vigilante matter of great significance. After being rebuffed several times, the senior agent finally consented, emphasizing that he could take no more than four days away from the office in Olympia, including the weekend. It was now Thursday morning and he would plan to be back on the job the following Monday.

His next call was to Interstate Airlines to make his flight arrangements and then a confirming call to Agent Jim Holcomb.

"Ok, Jim, I made a compelling case to the boss, and he let me go for Friday and the weekend. Have to be back here bright-eyed Monday morning, so cut yourself loose on Thursday night and my time is yours. We're gonna need a lot of coffee and privacy."

Holcomb gasped a reply of real gratitude. "Thanks, Charlie. I owe you big-time for this one, so put it on my tab. I can meet you at the airport and get you lodging at the Pistol Creek Motel, if that's OK."

"Jim, I am having trouble getting an exact flight confirmation and don't have any time left around here to mess with it. Suppose I just get there, rent a car and go to the motel on my own. I know you are up to your armpits with stuff too, so you won't have to worry about the details. I'll call you when I am at the motel. Is that OK?"

"Yep, Charlie, I'll be waiting for your call. See you then."

Moving hastily down a crowded corridor, Charles made a quick call on his personal cell phone. "Yes," he mumbled quietly, "same place at about 9:30 or so. Lots to discuss, so plan to spend the night." He was four minutes late for the "in progress" briefing in the corner conference room, feeling relieved that he could get to the bottom of the Montana vigilante affair and leave it in capable hands. He would explain as much as he dared to his wife, after the trip was over.

When his briefing was concluded, Gettys called two of his senior officers aside to advise them of his trip and give them the priorities that required their attention while he was away. The next twelve hours immersed him in a flurry of activity that took his mind off the pressing issue of the Justice Brigade. At some point, he managed a call to his wife to explain that he had a required trip the following day and suggested that they find a quiet restaurant for an evening dinner together. Her hours away from the *Olympia Register* were as limited as his.

The late dinner was a welcomed event for them both, and Wednesday morning greeted Charles with deep exhaustion from a sleepless night. In a blurred frame of mind, he made his way through check-in at Interstate Airlines and soon found himself in a deep sleep as the little commuter airplane made its way to Montana. He slept through the intermediate stops en-route and awoke with a shudder when he was aroused for the landing in Butte. Breathing deeply to clear his mind, he made his way to the car rental desk and signed for a black SUV.

A September chill was in the quiet, night air and every star stood out starkly in the intense blackness overhead. The SUV's headlights illuminated tiny sparkles of light that danced on frosted range grass and sage brush as he drove quietly up to the old way station known as Spook Davis' Grub and Tail Roost.

CHAPTER 19
Sweeping Up The Pieces

For unknown numbers of years, Spook's way station has been the meeting place and restful retreat for the Justice Brigade's supreme Council of Ten. On this chilly autumn night, the Council of Ten would be in emergency session.

The splash of headlights through the windows, click of the car door closing and footsteps creaking across the boards of the porch announced his arrival. He was the last to enter, and the rush of cold air from the opened door followed him into the warmth of the dimly lit room. "Evenin' gents! Saw the lights and thought I might drop in for a visit." He hung his hat and coat on the pegs beside the door as the others turned to recognize him.

The crackle of the wood fires inside and the wild, sweet odor of burning yellow pine comforted his senses. For an instant, he was transported back in time to memories of the smells he grew up with in the timbered mountains of Montana. All were there: crisp, clear reflections of campfires warming chilled hunting camps and the dull, red glow of wood stoves of winter in prospector cabins and ranch houses. Along with the visions came the echoes of old-timers telling tales of adventure, humor and tragedy.

The sensations were the pure gold of his Montana heritage and he had devoted his life to making their virtues last.

"Well, look who showed up. The coyotes howling out there was barely keeping us awake anyhow so we might as well BS a spell. How you been?" Handshakes all around and welcoming smiles greeted him warmly. A glass of whiskey was thrust to his hand, "Gnaw on this a while. Might keep the bedbugs off."

There were eight men present, standing randomly around the central dining table, the cook stove and fireplace. Each wore a sidearm ranging in vintage from Colt .45 *Peacemaker Model* through various double action revolvers and the modern Glock semi-auto. Badges of various shapes glistened from left breast pockets or waist belts. The one common adornment in evidence was a tiny gold ring on the right little finger of each, that occasionally emitted a glint of light from the Yogo sapphire mounted in its center.

"Thanks. I guess one of our number is missing, Brig Johnson, and I hope he's doing OK over there in your jail, Roy."

"Yep, good old Brig is making it just fine and almost has control of the place, heh heh."

The leader spoke to bring things to order, "Brothers, we have some very serious and demanding work at hand because things have gotten kinda complicated here for a bit. We are here to work out some plans to fix 'em up and Charles has some ideas to bounce off you so pitch in at any time with your ideas so that there aren't any loopholes."

Charles began, "Anyone's thoughts and schemes are mighty welcome. Ben, you're our treasurer, so I want to make sure you can handle wire transfers of money to anyone here who needs it because this could get a little expensive in spots. Get account numbers from each of us before we get out of here. OK?"

Ben answered, "Yep. From wills, endowments and contributions over the years, we have over $280,000 banked. An easy assignment if that's enough money, but I can use a little more responsibility if you have some to spare."

"I think we will all have our platters full," he replied. "Seems to me that we have about three large orders to fill here, and you guys speak up if you have anything to add. First is to clean up the battlefield and take care of jobs undone. Second, I believe we need our own witness protection program, and I have worked out some details on that. We have some of our own folk to put into that program and we will make it happen soon, before any of this 9-11 tidal wave gets people thinking about other things to do. Third, we have to eliminate a key witness, and fourth, take care of the aftermath and bathtub rings."

Another voice came from near the fireplace, "That's a fairly good outline, so why don't you go ahead and delegate, and we'll try to fill in the gaps."

The leader spoke, "So, as to unfinished business, who we got on hand that needs finishin'?"

Mineral County Deputy Sheriff, Chub Denton, spoke up. "I have Jeep Rogers up in the old Bearcat Mine and Eddie Weeks at the Quartz City ghost town. 'Bout time we took care of them for good. I think I can draft four of our own as helpers from Missoula and Ravalli counties."

"OK, you are going to have to make that happen, nice, clean, permanent, and soon. Who else?"

Bannack Sheriff Pickett cleared his throat and spoke. "I've had that damned Tennessee Senator Ashford Lee Keller out there in my jail for near three months now and haven't had the time or help to put him away proper. I'm gettin' too old for grave digging and wrestling people around for the noose."

The leader turned to Bozeman Police lieutenant, William Mosure. "Bill, can you arrange to go over to Bannack and help Pickett and his deputy do their duty?"

Mosure answered, "Yep. Sooner the better for me. Bill, you just let me know when it's convenient and I will be there."

"Ok, if that's all we have, we're done with those three." He then addressed Joe Brown of the U.S. Marshall Service. "So we have one more to take care of and I guess you are the only one who might know where he is, right Joe?"

"I guess you are talking about Reamy Nelson, right?" said Joe. The leader nodded and Brown continued, "I got his ID papers and stuff for the protection program and shipped him off to Kenneth, Utah. We can't go through the service to get more information without tipping our hand, but I may be able to do some long distance research to find him. I'll let you know. Then what?"

"Well, if we really want to clean things up for good, Nelson will have to be eliminated, no matter where he is. It's kinda too bad about Nelson. He was a loyal and dedicated young officer, completely naïve and innocent. Unfortunately, he's also the kind of guy who will never be able to understand why we exist.

"We should be thinking about operating from here on under the *no witness* theory of Montana justice. Always worked before and should do just fine nowadays. How about us drafting Officer Charlie Runner from over on the Crow Reservation to go hunting for Reamy? I think he would be perfect for the job. Joe, will you work with him on the details? We're going to need that done within the month."

"Sounds perfect to me," replied Brown."

Charles added to Brown, "We are also going to need seven complete identity packages, one female that will fit for Anita, and six others matching our guys in the Butte jail. We have to get to our man in the Marshal's service for them. Can you fix that?"

"Yep. No problem. I'll have that done within the week."

Charles directed his next comments to Captain Harold Miller of the Montana Highway Patrol. "I'm going to have to be away for some time before we get this done, so I would like to have you take charge locally to coordinate things. Can you do that for us? I will surely be involved out here for the windup and pitch in if anything should go wrong."

"Sure," replied Miller. "Consider it done and I will report back to you from time to time in Olympia on how things are going."

"Thanks, Harold. Your first responsibility will be to get the ID packages from Joe and have them ready for the big day. Get word to the prisoners and have them convert every asset they have into cash. Harold, you will also need to get those cash packages together for each because they will surely need all the money they can take with them. They're all going to require new duds too.

"So, we have ID stuff figured out, and I think I can commit to placements for each of them. There's a good chance of arranging a trial attorney's job for Anita Martin, I mean her alias, in River Port, South Dakota. I'm sure I can place the other six into law enforcement outfits in Idaho, eastern Oregon and Washington State. I also have some ideas about getting our folks from here to there.

"Gentlemen, we have some real logistical hurdles to get over, and the most critical piece of our work is timing. We will have no rehearsals and will have to coordinate things on time, right down to the cat's whisker."

Henry Lowell from Virginia City interrupted, "About timing. What kind of deadline are we dealing with? Besides, I need something to do, so be sure to count me in. I'm not yet too old to play a hand or two."

"Thanks, Henry, I was about to get into our timing, and I was going to point a finger at you. Roy, you have the jail and the prisoners, and your guys get them back and forth for hearings at the federal courthouse, right? So, when is the next hearing that requires their presence?"

The Silver Bow sheriff replied "Let me see now. I think it's on Friday, October 12 at 9:00 A.M. I'm pretty sure of that, but will confirm at the office and get back to Harold on it."

"OK, so there's our deadline, gentlemen, Charles emphasized, "Barely three weeks from now, and we have a lot to do. Roy, call on Judge Smith and ask him not to get upset about the prisoners missing their appointment until, let's say, about one hour after they are supposed to be in his court. It's in that hour that we must operate, guys. It all goes down between 9:00 and 10:00 on Friday, October 12. Any change to that will come from Harold, and we will all go with it.

"Your department provides the feds with an evidence locker for everything involving our case. After this goes down, everything in it disappears: depositions, bones, autopsies, trash bags . . . everything! The same goes for the judge. The paperwork on these proceedings goes away, accidental fire or whatever. It all vanishes."

"We will find a way and make it happen," replied the sheriff.

"Fine. And one more important thing, Roy. On our deadline morning, you will have to work out a day off or something for your jailers. You have a deputy who is one of ours, so arrange for you two guys to replace them. During that critical hour, you do a bit of stagecraft and later take falls after being overpowered by our seven "thugs". It has to be set up so that they can leisurely walk on out to the bus. Just take a little nap and when you wake up it will all be over. Haa-haa."

"Sounds workable to me, but more curious as we get into it," grinned the sheriff. "I'm afraid to ask what other weird ideas you have to spring on us."

"OK, Henry, now for you. Two important things, so let me know if you can't make them happen. One, get hold of a school bus real legal like and have it waiting near the courthouse in Butte by 9:00 A.M. that day. Two, get to our Highway Patrolman, Dan Davis, and have him standing by in the same area with his cruiser to transport one of our own to the Butte airport."

He then spoke to Lieutenant John Lake of the Kalispell Police Department. "John, does our Sheriff up there still have custody of Jeep Roger's commuter jet?

If we can get someone to fly it, I think we can use it."

Lake came back, "Yes, the plane is still parked at the Bigfork airport but may need some fuel and preflight stuff, whatever. I think I can arrange that. We also have a member with the Border Patrol at Eureka who is a former Air Force jet jockey. He says he can fly anything, so we might as well find out about that. I will get with him and report to Harold on it all."

"OK, John, that's a big order and I appreciate you taking care of it. If the snatch of the jet is a "go", arrange with the pilot to have it at the Butte airport by our deadline, ready for a quick flight to River Port, South Dakota. The flight will have to be "black bag" for the traffic control folks, so work out the alias stuff with him. You guys work out what is best to do with the aircraft afterwards."

"You've got it," Lake replied.

"Now, another little chore for our treasurer. Ben, before this all gets together, I want you to do some shopping for special garments that our prisoners will need and give them to Henry. Henry, after you park the bus, take the garments inside to Roy.

"Harold, we have to very secretly get to the prisoners to let them know about our little witness protection program. I don't think it is necessary that they know the exact time, but we must assure them that they will be taken care of, along with their families. I am thinking that we may be able to have them all back together within six months. That means explaining the same to the families; however our folks want it done. Ok?"

"I will see to it," replied Captain Miller.

"Well, guys, you now have my concepts. Let's take a break before we go to work picking them to pieces and drilling into the details."

Henry Lowell broke in again, "Hey, you got things worked out for where the airplane goes, but you haven't said anything about the bus. Where do I go with the bus?"

"Ha! Henry, you aren't going to have to drive the bus more than a mile from the jail house and your destination is my little secret for now. This is gonna be one of the fanciest jail breaks you ever heard of, and I am saving that part for a big surprise. I will fill you in on that one later."

The deep voice of their leader interrupted, "Brothers, we have outlined a whirlwind of complex activities for the largest jail break I have ever heard of. Let me summarize and we'll take a break.

"We have the means of getting new identities for our seven criminals, a date and time to get them out of jail and the means of transporting them away from Butte. One will fly to South Dakota and the rest will be in our custody. It all goes down on October 12 at 09:00 A.M. with no errors. Miller here will be our communications and control and I will be handling our checklist to fill in any gaps or give whatever support we need. If any of you need money to pull this off, call Ben and he will transfer to your accounts whatever you need. Harold, I see you have also been tending to that big coffee pot on the stove and I am sure ready for some."

"Yep," Harold spoke. "Should go down pretty good with the sandwiches I have out in my rig. Henry brought along a big bunch of home-made buffalo jerky in that paper bag over there, so I think we are set for the night."

An instant rumble of small talk and joking ensued as the men began their snacks. Coffee cups were filled and some of the attendees moistened their glasses with generous charges of Canadian whiskey or scotch. They consumed their refreshments leisurely, but there was an air of urgency to get their task completed. With the meal finished, the large warm room again filled with tobacco smoke as the men quietly entered into serious questions and debates on each item of the plan that had been outlined for them.

They worked on through the night under the glow of oil lamps. These were professional veteran lawmen who were thoroughly focused and committed to complex tasks and assignments, although not a note was taken. Each responsibility and increment of the plan was committed to memory.

In the hour before dawn, they finalized the plan, and without mention from anyone, began clearing the trash, washing cups and dishes, refilling the lamps with kerosene, and preparing to carry out the ashes from the dying fires. Someone murmured quietly, "Always leave a camp bettern ya found it." It was one of the codes of the old west that Montana natives had been taught from the time they learned to walk.

Midmorning, Charles met with Holcomb and listened as he poured forth his suspicions about others in law enforcement and ideas for busting up the entire Justice Brigade. However, it seemed that Holcomb's investigations continued to fall short. He could get no one to verify anything! He was very frustrated and welcomed Charles' listening ear.

As Charles sat seemingly engaged in Holcomb's ideas, he became more certain that the Brigade's plan actually could work. Here was evidence of a proven lawman who could find absolutely no answers and had absolutely no real plan in hand that could bring down the JB. The Brigade definitely had the upper hand!

After spending many hours with Jim, Charles assured him that once he could find a few open days, he would do some investigating of his own and see what he might do that would help Holcomb's case against those who were already jailed as alleged JB members. Jim was happy to hear this, but was stunned when Charles expressed his concerns that they may never find anyone who could or would substantiate the suspicions that Jim had. It could all turn into a dead end, but for now, they would concentrate on who they already had and the evidence they were compiling against them. If the suspects would cooperate for leniency or plead out for lesser charges, maybe they would bring others down with them.

CHAPTER 20

One Witness

Kenneth, Utah, is a typical Mormon farm community with a population of 4,563 earnest, hard working souls situated in the flat, well-nurtured agricultural country north of Ogden. It lies some 30 miles west of the Interstate Highway with a geographic remoteness that is matched by the attitude of the community. Not much new happens in Kenneth and that is the way its citizens like it.

But progress had made its way into Kenneth, such as it has everywhere else in America. Kenneth is proud of its new farm and implement store, an expanded Safeway and several new drive-ins and convenience stores. One of the newest had been recently purchased by Alan Smith, a pleasant young man with a quiet, almost anti-social wife. The Smiths had easily adapted to the friendliness of the town and its sedate ways, and both were studying to become members of the Church of Jesus Christ of Latter Day Saints.

Before registering in the Twin Star Motel two days earlier, Charlie Runner had rented a car in Milad on his way to Kenneth from Montana. He had been visited at Crow Agency by U.S. Marshall Joe Brown, and they had a private discussion about the errand the Justice Brigade had assigned to Runner that required his trip to Kenneth. His boss at Crow Agency made no objection to his taking a needed week from work to join an elk hunting camp with friends over in the Patomac area. The leave was granted and Charlie left without delay for Utah, carrying $1,000 in expense money given to him in cash by Brown.

Assuming the role of a real estate agent scouting properties, Runner moved easily around Kenneth and was virtually unnoticed as he scanned through courthouse records of recent residence and business sales. On the first day, he concluded that he had found what he was looking for. It was the Lucky Convenience Market, purchased a month before by Channel Investment Associates, and a residence at 234 Park Street, obtained by the same company.

The records showed no subsequent transfers and no other names were recorded as owners. Ha! Runner mused. The previous owners probably never listed the properties for sale or even knew they were for sale. But they were. Everything has its price, and the U.S. Treasury has unlimited resources.

After breakfast, Charlie drove to the convenience store and shopped around for a few minutes until he felt sure that the person behind the counter was the one he was looking for. He approached to check out his goods, thrust out his hand and said, "Hello, I'm Stan Baker. Are you new here?"

The man returned his handshake and replied with a smile, "Alan Smith. My wife and I just moved here and are happy to get acquainted with new people from around the area."

"Then welcome! It's always a pleasure to meet new folk, and I hope you like Kenneth. Have a good day." Charlie picked up his change and returned to his rental car. In a few minutes, he was in touch with a telephone operator who confirmed that they had a new listing for the Smiths at 234 Park Street. Runner had found his prey. From then on, he closely observed Smith to find the best opportunity to approach him alone. That meeting would be decisive and final.

By carefully studying Smith's routines over the following two days, Runner learned that the convenience store opened at 8:00 each morning and closed at 8:00 P.M. Smith always drove to the Green Pastures Cafe each morning before work and had breakfast there at 7:00. He carried a well-used manila envelope that held register and inventory paperwork, which he worked on each day at a remote booth where he would not be disturbed. On the third day of his visit, Charlie Runner sat down to have breakfast with Smith in his booth.

Smith smiled and greeted him, "Uh you're Mr. Baker, right?"

"Yes, I'm Baker," Charlie responded in a cool tone of voice as he placed on the table between them a simple little gold ring with a blue sapphire set between the characters "JB".

The color drained from Smith's face and he gasped, "You're here!"

"Yes, Reamy, we are here. Now, listen to me very carefully," he spoke quietly and precisely. "You are someone the organization wants permanently and completely eliminated, both you and your wife. But if I was going to kill you, I wouldn't be here talking about it over your breakfast, would I?"

"N-n-o, I—I guess not," stuttered Smith.

The waitress appeared with a cup and poured coffee for Smith and Runner, asking Charlie if he wanted to order breakfast. He politely declined.

Charlie continued, "You are here under a federal protection program that has failed you. The Justice Brigade has the only witness protection program that is really worth anything, and you are going to be part of it. You are going to pay your dues right here and now, Reamy, and you are never going to stray from the rules again in your life.

"Utah is a very clandestine environment and this is a small town. You belong here or you don't, and you are accepted or not, in the opinion of the Church. The Church knows everything, and you will never escape that fact. Naturally, our organization has ways to make good use of their mechanism to do what is right and proper for the people here. Do you understand that, Reamy?"

"Yes. I know you are right. I know that is how you found me. I just didn't imagine that you would have ties down here," whispered Smith.

"You don't really know anything about the organization, Reamy, and that is the only benefit we might have in letting you live. And whatever you did know about the JB is now completely erased from your little brain cells. Is that clear?"

"Yes, sir."

Runner went on, "You are the only witness to what went on at Timberline. You are the only one who can condemn seven solid, loyal and dedicated souls to their death. Your testimony is vital to their trial, and now you have nothing ever to say about what you saw or learned in Montana.

"This means that, once again in your life, you are going to betray an outfit that really needs your commitment and that is exactly what you will do. As a result, they will dump you out of their program and you will be alone. Without us, you would be out there on your own, maybe once again as Reamy Nelson, for all they could care. But you are either in our witness protection program, or you become just another dirty little job in our dead witness program.

"There is no escape from where you now are. It is not a choice; it is a fact that you will live with forever. You will convince your wife about every word of what I am saying and this arrangement will never be discussed with the children of your future life, your grandchildren . . . no one! Ever! Failure means death, and we will know the instant you fail.

"Obey, Reamy, and you will make a new life here as Alan Smith. Let my words flow through your veins and never doubt them. Walk the straight path from here on, and you will have a rewarding life in Mormon country. I am through with you now, Alan Smith. Have a good day and thanks for the coffee."

Nelson shuddered as the lanky Indian rose and walked slowly to the door. The rental car with the Utah license plates soon backed out of its parking place and moved slowly onto the county road in front of the Green Pastures Cafe. Charlie had done his job and was now on his way back to Montana.

But the witness had left a paper trail behind him in Montana that must be eliminated. Cabinets in the Butte Federal Building were filled with Nelson's depositions, arraignment papers, and motion briefs from the newly-arrived Federal Attorney and lawyers representing the seven notorious suspects. The evidence locker under the custody of the Silver Bow County Sheriff contained boxes of material evidence gathered at the scene of their arrest, including the manacles that were worn by Reamy Nelson.

The clock was moving forward on the trial, one that would have made daily headlines had it not been for the overwhelming disaster of the terrorist bombings of September 11, 2001. That event, and America's response to it, continued to consume newspaper and television space throughout the planet. Even so, the Justice Brigade was watching the clock, steadily and precisely in motion toward each of its assigned objectives.

The morning after the secret JB conference, U.S. Marshall Harold Brown made contact with associates in the agency to obtain seven identity packages that were set up for the Federal Witness Protection Program. He would receive them by express mail within the week. On the same morning, Silver Bow County Sheriff, Roy Evans, made a call to his friend, Federal Judge Arthur Smith and arranged for a quiet appointment for dinner at a local restaurant. It was arranged early, before the place filled with customers and would provide a setting for discreet, leisurely conversation.

They arrived at the restaurant at nearly the same time and entered together, finding a private corner booth. After they ordered cocktails, Evans outlined the purpose of the meeting. "Judge, the JB is moving decisively on this Timberline mess and the fix is on. It will be complete, thorough and without a hitch. A good number of us have assignments and one includes you."

"Well," Smith responded, "I trust that whatever plan you have is one of great merit, considering the depth of experience you all represent. I have been on edge wondering if anything was going to come about because this case threatens a century of law and order in Montana that would never again be the same. In some respects, I have been thinking that rescuing the JB might be impossible."

"Well, it is perfectly possible, Judge. We are taking away all elements of the crimes, excepting the crime scene. Where there are no witnesses, no evidence, no depositions, no records, and no accused, it would seem impossible to prosecute anything. That is just where we are going with this plan."

"What kind of a bunch of rough-neck magicians do you think you guys are anyhow?" the judge scoffed. "You might as well try to make Mount Rushmore disappear!"

"Well, only one of us is completely aware of the separate pieces that go into making it all work, and that guy is as shrewd as anyone. You know who he is. My piece is to do away with physical evidence that I have stored away in the county evidence locker for your court and explain your part to you. You and I can find a way to make it work. Whatever sits in my custody on the case will wind up in some land-fill for sure, without any problems. We need to do the same with court records."

"Now you have me interested, Ben. Are you serious about making those seven defendants vanish?"

"Yep, and a lot more. So, here is how your part works out. You know where all the records are pertaining to this case, right?"

"Yes, I have control over what is there and where. Many files are duplicated, but all are registered and accounted-for. That is, all except those in the hands of the defense attorneys. We have one out-of-state attorney defending, one from Bozeman and three from Butte. They have their own files of records on the case. As for our office, my clerk has the master set of everything, and many are with the office of the U.S. Attorney. He is visiting here, so I doubt that he takes anything home to his apartment."

"OK, Judge, please get the names and addresses of the defense attorneys to me tomorrow, if possible. You have a hearing on this case coming up on your calendar for 9:00 A.M on October 12. Don't let anyone change that date. Between now and then, records have to begin to disappear, and all of them have to be gone by that morning. On that day, don't get upset if your defendants are a little late for appearance. You will never see them again, but trust that they will be well cared-for under our own witness protection program. What kind of help do you need to deal with the disposal of case records?"

"Ben, that's a big order, but let me think out loud on it for a few minutes. There is a lot of bulk in those records and when nothing is going on, no one usually goes into them. I don't think older files would be missed if they kind of started getting lost or something. I can make visits to my clerk's filing system at night and get a lot of that done before the final night. Then I might need some help purging all of it.

"As for the U.S. Attorney's records, he doesn't keep all of what I have and therefore, his files would probably be less bulky. We would need a stealthy helper to work on that one at night. We need keys. Let me see . . .

"Hey, Ben, I think I have it! After Anita was arrested at Timberline, a warrant was issued to search her residence. In the boxes of seized items, there should be keys to her office and all of the filing cabinets in there. Check them out."

"Right, Judge! I went through all of that stuff searching for little JB rings so that people wouldn't come up with an idea that there might be some gigantic secret conspiracy associated with those symbols. I picked up several rings and remember seeing a bunch of keys in Anita's things. I'll go through the inventory lists and find them for sure."

"OK Ben. So, do you have someone who can get in there appropriately?"

"Sure. That would be me," the sheriff chuckled.

The Judge went on, "Well, that takes care of the records in our hands. What about those with the defense attorneys?"

"That is going to be simple burglary, your honor. We have members in Bozeman and Butte who can take care of that,

I'm sure. There will have to be surveillance to determine just where the records are kept and what would be needed to make them disappear on the last night. I will know three days in advance if there are any problems or unknown factors, but we are going ahead with the deadline, regardless. All I need to know is who and where they are."

"I will have that to you tomorrow."

"Now comes the Academy Award show, Judge."

"What do you mean, Ben?"

"I mean that you are going to have to be the most convincing actor of all time when you handle the aftermath. The press will be on the courthouse like ugly on an ape! You are going to have to piss and moan and throw a real conniption fit about this horrendous atrocity, this ghastly assault on the federal court. I can see you screaming about catching every last one of the bastards who pulled this off!" the sheriff was laughing aloud.

The judge laughed in reply, "That shouldn't be a big problem. Most of my work on the bench over the years has been a big act anyhow."

Steak dinners and a nightcap followed before they retired.

The following day, Sheriff Evans received a call from the judge's secretary who reported the names and addresses of the defense attorneys to him. He quickly called the project coordinator, Captain Harold Miller of the Montana

Highway Patrol and arranged for a hamburger lunch at the Flying "J'" in Rocker. After he had delivered the requirements to him for the burglaries, he was assured that the right people would be assigned and they would report any problems three days before the deadline. Afterward, Evans made his way to his county jail to make a customary visit to the inmates.

With each of the seven Timberline suspects, he paused to deliver a very important message. "You must get word to your spouse, trustee or anyone responsible for your property to convert everything to cash. Make out powers of attorney if necessary. Get them busy liquidating anything worth a buck. I mean homes, cars, books, toys, guns, boats, bikes, excess clothing, tools, and furniture. They have barely two weeks to get it all done. Cook up yard sales, auctions, hardship sales of any kind. Such activity should not gather much notice since your kin folks are bound to need money to pay for your defense.

"I cannot tell you right now that a big event is planned and you will learn about it soon. If any of your next of kin cannot be ready by then to move away in a minute's notice, you are not to tell them anything. They will be cared-for later on and should not be able to give anything away in an inquisition. You must let me know in next two days who goes and who remains."

His advice was acknowledged by everyone without question. By evening, the judge had called to report that he had some paper to dispose of.

CHAPTER 21

Dancing In The Moonlight

The western third of Montana is a region of high, abrupt mountains with lush evergreen forests intersected by swift, crystal-clear, mountain streams. Over the last century, the National Forests in Montana have been the source of massive timber harvesting and yields of lumber that continue today. Hundreds of square miles of un-touched forests remain and second harvests have renewed production on older, re-grown tracts. The richness of the mountain region and its people still mirrors the character of the rugged, sparsely populated Montana frontier of earlier days and this identity will remain in place far into the future.

The nature of timber work has not changed over the years, but the tools and machines that build roads, take down the trees, and bring the logs to the sawmills have altered the industry immensely from the days of horse and oxen implements. Modern chain saws, giant bulldozers, backhoes, tram lines, skidders and powerful trucks have brought machine power and efficiency to the formerly back-breaking work of the early day timber jacks.

In hundreds of logging sites in the area west of Missoula, new harvesting has entered into the higher mountains above old cutting in the lower elevations. They are places of roughly hewn access roads, temporary stream crossings, and gouged-out skid roads and trails. The workplaces are saturated with unnatural smells of diesel smoke combined with the odors of freshly churned virgin earth, pine needles, and crushed evergreen cuttings. As it has for generations, logging work begins at daybreak and ends at sundown. In the mountains, the contrast between daylight and night is sudden and dramatic. Operating areas are a noisy bustle by day and deserted at night. Heavy equipment is left unattended in the remoteness of the locale, randomly parked along the rutted new tracks where the machines can be fueled and serviced.

In one such place, a black night of intense mountain silence had fallen upon the upper reaches of Chokecherry Creek and its sparkling little tributary streams. Near the hour of 2:00 A.M, on a pre-determined October morning, bright headlights appeared, knifing through the darkness, bouncing and twisting through the rough terrain and splintering stark shadows through the standing trees. A pickup truck and two SUVs approached the end of the rutted logging access road and quietly halted in a loose semi-circle beside a large, silent backhoe.

They had gathered at a place where the road left the highway and Chokecherry Creek joins the Clark Fork River, each from a different direction and arriving at slightly different times. Into the night, they made up a small convoy as they journeyed the last 25 miles to the end of the road. One SUV was driven by Mineral County Deputy Sheriff, Chub Denton, assisted by a JB member of the Montana Highway Patrol. In their custody is the condemned California murderer, Jeep Rogers.

Ravalli constable Clay Mitchell drove the other SUV with a JB helper who sat beside a manacled man in the back seat. Their cargo is the molester and child murderer, Eddie Weeks. The pickup truck carried two other JB lawmen from Missoula who had been chosen to help on the upcoming event.

When they reached their destination, the headlights remained on while the officers left their vehicles, stretched and moved about to gather fire wood. One of the group walked purposefully over to the backhoe and climbed aboard. A few seconds later the steel monster groaned, let out a long whine and eased into a low, murmuring idle. In the next minute, the operator had the long arm moving and its digging bucket scratching into the rocky spoils on the right margin of the crude road. There, beneath the slope of the hillside, a trench parallel to the road began to take shape under the headlight beams of the parked vehicles. Choked sobs and whining could be heard from inside both the SUV's.

In the middle of the road, the blaze of a new fire grew while the little gathering chatted in low tones. One went to his pickup to retrieve a bottle of Jack Daniels which was passed around the group. Each took a generous sip. The bottle passed once around and was taken back to the pickup and a length of new hemp rope was brought from its cargo bed into the headlights. One of the Missoula lawmen began forming one end of the rope into the familiar hangman's noose bound by a tight coil of thirteen wraps. When the first knot was finished, he paced off an estimate of required length, cut the rope and tied another noose. With the two nooses held together, he found the middle of the rope and formed a loop knot. His work done, the lawman moved close to the fire to wait for next part of the night's project to unfold.

Two of the men ambled over to the excavation which had grown to nearly four feet deep. "A few more passes, Clay, and that should do it. I don't think we will need all six feet for their miserable carcasses. When you think the trench is deep enough, reach that boom over the road about there and let me tie the loop over the bucket. When I give you the word, jerk the arm upward about four feet and that should do it. Ok. Let's get our honored guests out here guys."

As they returned to the two SUV's, others joined them. "Time for a stretch break for you, Jeep. You've been cooped up in one place or another for quite a while." The sobbing from inside the SUV's had broken into loud wailing and deep, guttural pleas for mercy. The lawmen lunged inside and forcibly pulled each of the two manacled prisoners out of the vehicles and to their feet. Neither could remain standing and they slumped onto the loose dirt of the road. "I never thought you would kill me!" shouted Rogers.

"Hell, Jeep, you were tried and sentenced right after we found out you were in Montana. We just kept you around long enough for the vision of your dirty, rotten crimes to seep into your brain," answered one of the shadowy figures standing over him. "Whew! Jeep, you smell something awful! You having bowel problems?"

Eddie Meeks writhed in the dirt, loudly crying and pleading for his life. "Don't kill me! For God's sake, let me live! Please let me live, I don't want to die! I'm not ready to die!" Another of the shadowy witnesses spoke up, "Eddie, that little girl you raped and stabbed to death. Did she cry for mercy or have a chance to plead for her life? Bawl all you want to, Eddie. It might make up for what you denied to her in the last moments of her life. Feel good about that, Eddie, for now you are in the last moments of yours."

Two men on either side of the prone figures tried to stand them upright but failed. The prisoners collapsed limply onto the ground and remained writhing there, racked by deep sobbing. Deputy Mitchell spoke, "Couple of you guys see if you can rustle up two skinned out pieces of lodgepole from the spoils over the bank there. We need them six feet or longer.

"Boys, it looks like we are going to have to do this the old fashioned way from back when those big, brave outlaws turned too yellow to face their own Maker standing up like men. We have a couple of goddamned cowards here just like them, and we are going to need some extra pieces of rope and duct tape or whatever."

Within minutes, two men returned with poles and the others came forward with pieces of rope and tape. "Roll them birds out flat on their bellies, boys," said Mitchell. "Then bind the poles tight down their spines and leave about six inches past their shoes. Hog tie them real good, and then we will stand them up."

When the grappling with prisoners and poles was finished, the men at the side of each prisoner lifted them upright about two feet apart. They were propped into an upright position with the butts of the poles preventing their feet from touching the ground. Mitchell held a rope with a noose at each end and motioned for the backhoe boom and fastened its center over two teeth on the bucket. "Ok, Bill, just move that bucket right above their heads and I will add the finishing touches."

The backhoe arm swung to the left and paused about four feet over the heads of the prisoners. Mitchell stepped up to each of them and fastened the nooses, making sure that the knot coils were positioned below their right ears and resting on their shoulders. He backed away to the center of the road, facing the vehicle headlights. "Jeep Rogers and Eddie Weeks, you have been tried and convicted by the good citizens of Montana for the crimes of bloody murder. Sentence will now be carried out and you will hang by your necks until you are dead. May your evil souls forever burn in Hell."

He signaled with a motion of his left hand and the backhoe arm jumped upward. In an instant, the slack of the ropes disappeared and the two condemned men were jerked aloft, bumping into each other. Slight twitching of their knees and feet gave evidence that they died instantly. The men who had held them upright paused briefly and then faced each other, shaking hands all around. "Leave them hangin' a few minutes while we have another snort of 'Jack', boys," Mitchell said. Someone moved to retrieve the bottle.

Through distant trees over a ridge top, the bright whiteness of a rising moon appeared as the fire's glow cast the moving shadows of the prisoners upon the steep road bank walls. In the slight mountain breeze, the joined images moved in unison and twisted slowly in a macabre waltz.

As the two shadows embraced and danced under the moonlight, the bottle was passed around and offered to the backhoe operator. Clay finished it off and trashed it in the waiting trench. "Well, that just about takes care of those two filthy murderers. Clay, swing them around and dump them into that hole. As soon as you get the dirt over them, we'll all head on out of here together. We did a good piece of work here tonight, fellas, and I'm proud to be here with you."

The backhoe arm swung to the right and the suspended prisoners were guided and dropped into the waiting trench. The boom turned back with the bucket extended and eased down to scratch up the remains of the fire which were also deposited into the excavation. Then, the careful process of grading the bucket from side to side across the loose spoils beside the trench began. It was soon filled and the operator put the machine into gear and moved it forward, running the right track the length of the filled trench and compacting the earth beneath it. It remained there when the engine was shut off and the operator dismounted. Quietly, the men returned to their vehicles, turned them around in the limited space of the logging road and the little procession slowly departed.

On the following night, at a place some two hundred miles to the southeast, the Justice Brigade had another execution to perform. It would take place in the rolling, barren foothills of the Lemhi Mountains near the old ghost town of Bannack. There, in the custody of Sheriff Sam Pickettt, was the condemned former Secretary of Agriculture, Ashford Lee Keller from Tennessee. Keller had been publicly accused of the murder of his mistress, but no evidence of his complicity was ever developed by the authorities. Months of investigations yielded no leads and the body of Jamie Rae Knight was never found.

National media attention was focused on the mystery for nearly a year and had begun to subside, but it was all re-awakened when Secretary Keller disappeared.

The search into his whereabouts revealed that he had flown to Helena, Montana, stayed six days and returned to Nashville. Eye witnesses from the press and television media positively identified him arriving at the Nashville airport. They saw him leave and enter a rental car shuttle, never to be seen again in Tennessee. That's because he never returned to Tennessee. He was a prisoner in Bannack, Montana, awaiting execution in a little stone jail cell. The mystery of his baffling absence was a plot perfectly crafted by the Justice Brigade that would never be unraveled.

At 11:00 P.M. Keller was awakened by the sounds of keys clanking at his cell door and the squeal of the door's movement. "Time to wake up, Mr. Secretary. We will be leaving this place for a while."

He groaned, sitting upright on his iron cot, "What is it Sheriff? What's going on?"

"Get your pants on, Mr. Keller, and here's a jacket. It's a little chilly tonight," said the Sheriff.

His hands were carefully pulled behind him and he was handcuffed before being led out of the little jail into the headlights of two waiting vehicles. Three silent men were standing close by in the darkness. "Why do we have to leave in the middle of the night, Sheriff?"

"Well, Mr. Keller, let's just say we have an appointment to make. We'll be taking a little drive, so I will help you into the back seat of that Explorer over there. A couple of helpers are here if you need assistance, so don't get spunky."

"Oh, my God! This can't be! Sheriff, are you going to take me out there . . . is this it?"

"Yep, I'm afraid so, Mr. Secretary. Nobody intended for you to stay here forever, and we sure as hell aren't about to send you back to Tennessee. Let's get goin'."

Keller was gasping in short breaths as he shuffled along the dusty path. "Sheriff, when you arrested me, you said that I had been sentenced to life in prison. What has happened? I thought you lawmen out here had some principles, like honesty and fairness. You can't be taking me out to execution!"

"Well, Mr. Keller, the verdict I told you about was true, but I didn't tell you the second part of it to keep you from doing something risky or foolish that could get people hurt. You see, you were sentenced to life in prison, and you have been in my prison until this night. And this night is the end of your life. The jury also added a hanging to make sure you have completed your sentence. Does that fix things up a bit about our good and honest character?" he asked with a chuckle.

He was helped into the rear of the SUV and soon it was bouncing and rocking slowly along an unused dirt road. Its headlights and those of the following pickup thrashed nervously across clumps of sage brush that quickly appeared, then disappeared into the darkness. The odors of dry, clay dust and sage filled the interiors of the vehicles as they worked their way along the rutted track. In the company of the Sheriff and his deputy, Keller remained silent but could not control his quiet sobbing. Between sniffles and whimpers, he could be heard mumbling prayers to the All Mighty. "Sheriff, you know you are going to hang an innocent man. You will become a murderer in your own right and earn the same kind of punishment you are about to give me. Please, Sheriff, don't do this crime! Let me live and serve the life of a prisoner, but don't kill me!"

"Lissen here, Keller. You and I have been through this discussion since you first came to my jail. It is always the same and this is the last time I am going to give you the facts. You are not innocent! You are only innocent until you are proven guilty in a court of law, and you have been found guilty in our court of law. That's it! Now, let me give you a little advice about your crime.

"You are getting damned close to drawing your last breath on this earth. In my opinion, the wisest thing you could ever do, in the limited time you have to do it, would be to admit what ever you have done and come clean with the Maker. The way I understand it is that you hafta do that before you leave here and not afterwards. That has a lot to do with where you will have to serve your eternities, and I suppose you have a little speck of religion in you somewhere. Give yourself a break! You have to admit this thing and be honestly and deeply sorry in your heart for what you have done. Then, when you pass on, you might be allowed to argue it all out up there and maybe get a probationary sentence or whatever. So, why not just lean back there and let it all out? What do you have to lose?"

A long silence followed before Keller drew a deep breath and began to tell his story. "Yes, Sheriff, you are my witness and God is my witness here and now. I did kill that beautiful little woman. I am deeply, honestly and painfully sorry for the great sin I have committed. I loved Jamie Rae and never meant to harm her. It is just that my anger and fright overwhelmed me, and I lashed out against her. I tried to end our affair and she blew up saying she would ruin me forever by writing a book and spilling all of our little intimacies and everything. She was a threat to the highest ambitions a man could have. I was planning to run for President of the United States and she would have trashed everything."

"And how did you do it Mr. Secretary?" asked Pickett.

Deeply sobbing, he continued, "I picked her up in the evening and we drove out on a remote country road where we could be alone. I had a rental car to prevent us being discovered and recognized. We talked, argued and I lost control of things. I pulled out my pocket knife and tried to stab her in the heart. I tried repeatedly but it must have been too small. She just slumped there weakly but still alive. I jumped out of the car, ran around to her side, pulled her out of the car by her hair and dragged her to the roadside. Then I cut her throat and she died."

Calmly, almost reverently, Pickett asked for more. "Well, Mr. Keller, what did you then do with her body?"

"My mind was in panic! I was almost delirious with fear and fright! I figured that she could be identified by her head and skull and wanted to cover that by cutting it off and concealing it separately from her body."

"You cut off her head with a little pocket knife?"

"Yes, right there in the grass beside the road. I don't know how I did it, but I do know that I had to work feverishly to carve through bones and tissue, and finally it came off. Then, I got a tire iron from the trunk of the car and dug a little hole with it where I buried her head."

"What did you do with her body?"

"I took off her clothes and wiped the blood from her body. Then I placed her into the trunk of the car and turned back down the country road to where we had passed a hog farm. I parked near the fence where there was a large gathering of hogs and made sure no one was around. Then, I got her out of the trunk, took her over there and discarded her among them. After that, I found a secluded place off the road where people had dumped trash, and burned all her clothing."

"That explains why her remains were never found. I suppose you cleaned everything up in the car before you turned it in and there was no trail of evidence in it."

"Yes, they never learned I had rented a car that night."

Keller seemed to have regained composure by the time the vehicles came to a halt in a dry wash among a grove of cottonwood trees. "I feel better now that I have gotten it off my chest, Sheriff. I almost wish I had confessed at the start."

Pickett's deputy alighted from the SUV and stepped into the headlights of the trailing pickup truck. He began giving verbal and hand signals to the driver who carefully backed it up beneath the heavy, almost horizontal branch of an aged cottonwood tree. "That should do it!" he shouted. The truck halted and the occupants emerged. Out of the darkness, sounds could be heard of them placing wooden planks and moving things around in the truck cargo box. The lawmen finished by placing a wooden crate on the ground at the center of the open pickup bed and quickly produced two lighted kerosene lanterns.

In the headlights of the Explorer, the deputy threw a completed noose and rope over the cottonwood limb. He adjusted it above the truck bed on which a platform of planks was now revealed in the lantern light. The rough boards bridged across the sides of the truck and filled half the space forward near the cab. "We're all ready here, Sheriff," called the deputy.

"Ok, Mr. Secretary, I think we should mosey on over there to see what the guys have been up to. Let me give you another bit of advice about this little ceremony. The best thing you can do is stand up there like a brave man and not fall down having a little fit. When that kind of thing happens, you just strangle to death and it sometimes takes a while. I don't much care whether you strangle or not, but we try to keep this thing kind of painless and merciful. Thrashing around just ruins our preparations and makes a bad day out of it for everyone. Surely, you don't want to go out being choked to death so just keep quiet and let us have control of things. It won't be like the torturous mess you did to that little woman and you should be grateful for that."

"God Almighty, I am weak, I'm not ready, Sheriff! Oh, God save me! I have repented of my sins and I want to live!"

The Sheriff and his deputy reached inside the SUV and forcibly assisted the prisoner out and onto his feet. Together, they walked to the rear of the waiting pickup truck, and Pickett assisted Keller as he stepped up on the crate, into the truck bed and onto the platform. Sobbing, Keller continued his prayers, pleading to be spared. Pickett's deputy passed him the noose and it was carefully cinched around Keller's neck, the coil resting on his shoulder below his right ear. "Ok, you can tie it off to the tree, Carl. About this much slack should do just fine," said Pickett.

The Sheriff then stepped down from the rear of the truck into the lantern light. His deputy started its engine and it idled quietly as he faced and spoke to Keller, "Ashford

Lee Keller, you have been caught, tried and found guilty of the crime of horribly murdering little Jamie Rae Knight in Tennessee. I bear witness to your confession of this ugly deed and have no idea if you were sincere in your sorrow or not. All it did was make me sick. Maybe that will cut you some slack in the Hereafter, maybe it won't, and that's not for us mortal folks to know. Anyhow, I am telling you that the good citizens of Montana have sentenced you to hang by the neck until you are dead and that is what is going to happen right now. Good bye, Mr. Keller."

The engine accelerated and the truck lurched forward. Planks clattered into the metal bed and spilled to the ground. Keller was jerked sideways by the snap of the noose, then instantly dropped downward where his upright form swung within two feet of the ground. A bright, full moon had risen above the far mountains to faintly illuminate the quiet scene of gentle hills, sagebrush, cottonwoods and two parked vehicles. The lifeless form of Keller was now silhouetted against the single, brilliant spotlight of a distant planet as he gracefully turned and swayed in a solo ballet dance.

Someone broke out a thermos of coffee and the four men mumbled softly as they sipped their refreshments. When the cups were emptied and put away, Pickett spoke, "Well, fellers, this has been a pretty clean piece of work, and we have done our duty. We can put him back into the truck now and take him over to a dry wash about a hundred yards from here. Carl will come around tomorrow with his tractor blade and cover him up. The world has seen the last of Secretary Keller and good riddance. Let's pick up the planks and go home."

They moved quietly and swiftly to their last tasks and soon the moonlight illuminated a mirage of dust behind vehicles departing across the sage and wild grass of Montana's outback. Nature's stillness quickly descended to reclaim a place briefly disturbed by the intrusions of mankind. In the distance, a coyote howled to add final comment to a case now closed forever.

After his usual breakfast of bacon, eggs and pancakes at Ella's cafe, Pickett arrived at his office in Virginia City at 9:00 the next morning. The Sheriff had kept news clippings about the case of Secretary Keller and his missing secretary from the time the Justice Brigade captured Keller. Pickett placed the thick folder on his desk and began sorting through it; carefully examining each item to find what he hoped would be there. At length, he found what he was looking for. One short news item revealed the names of the parents of Jamie Rae Knight. Anxiously, he summoned his secretary.

"Alice, I have a little item that I hope you can research on your computer. Here are the names of a couple of folks in Nashville, Tennessee, that I would like to have an address for. Is there any way you can get that for me?"

"Sure, boss," she replied. "That shouldn't be a problem at all."

"Well, you don't need to make any calls to confirm it. Just the mailing address will do. Thanks."

In minutes, she returned a Post-It note with the address on it. Pickett then drew a lined yellow tablet from his center drawer and began writing with a ballpoint pen.

October 7, 2001

To you dear folks of Jamie Rae Knight:

My heart has been with you since your daughter disappeared, and I want to let you know that I have shared your sadness and worries about what happened to her.

I am a lawman in a place you will never know about. I have always wanted to do something that would put your minds at ease about her, and maybe give you some rest. Our ideas about justice would never be trusted if victims did not know it was a reality. That is why I am writing to you.

I can tell you with certainty that Jamie Rae is gone. She was not tortured or held captive anywhere and her remains have been destroyed. They cannot be recovered. She is surely in the hands of the All Mighty because her life was taken away from her by another before she was able to make her own way through it.

Jamie Rae was killed by Ashford Lee Keller, and you can now be sure that justice has been carried

*out to avenge his crime. I was with Mr. Keller
when he confessed everything about the killing
to me and I was with him when he drew his last
breath and was hanged.*

*Dear folks, let your minds and hearts now rest.
Justice has been carried out and, by accepting
this truth, I hope you will be able to set the
whole sad experience behind you and survive
in peace from now on.*

Sincerely,

Lawman

Pickett carefully folded the letter and placed it into an envelope which he addressed to the Knights in Tennessee. On a larger manila envelope, he carefully penned the address of an old Army buddy living in Stamford, Connecticut. Then, on a yellow Post-It, he added:

*Ed—Here is a letter I need a blind cover for.
Please mail it out for me.*

I hope you and family are all doing fine.

Pickett

The Post-It was applied to the Knight letter and sealed inside the manila envelope. With it in hand, Picket rose and made his way out of the office. "Alice, I have an urgent letter to mail at the Post Office and will be back in a few minutes."

CHAPTER 22
A Memorable Anniversary Adventure

FBI Special Agent in Charge, Charles Gettys, found a significant backlog awaiting his return to the Olympia office. He was exhausted after his hurried trip to Montana but lunged determinedly into current issues and the stack of paperwork that had accumulated during his absence. His concentration was continually interrupted by thoughts of the intricate responsibilities that remained on the shoulders of his Justice Brigade friends in Montana. As well, he had returned with his own mental list of things to do with very little time to accomplish them. He felt sure, as the clock ticked away the minutes and hours, that pieces of the plans he had delegated were being carried out with professional skill and precision. The fabric that made up the official case of the "Timberline Seven" was beginning to disappear.

Charles' labors carried him forward through lunch and into the evening hours. In the afternoon, he found time to call his wife Janet, at the *Olympia Register,* to arrange a date for them to have dinner at their favorite seafood restaurant. It had a wonderfully relaxing atmosphere and a superbly crafted menu that would provide the perfect setting for his surprise.

Charles made time during the day to access the website of the Silver Empire tour train and confirm the booking he had made a week prior for an overnight trip for two on October 9. He made a quick phone call to his JB coordinator in Montana, making double-sure that reservations on the Silver Empire were confirmed for six other travelers. He learned that the number of special guests would be ten, counting helpers along the way. The departure date was just a few weeks away for Charles and Janet. He turned his attention to completing flight arrangements, and motel and auto reservations that would coincide with their travel adventure. Before he left work that evening, Charles had succeeded in getting everything prepared. Happily, he drove from the office, anxious to meet his wife and announce his anniversary plans.

Entering the restaurant, Charles found Janet in a secluded booth pouring two glasses of white table wine from a carafe. "Well," he said. "Are you expecting company?"

"Wow! You caught me!" she chuckled. "I guess you will have to substitute for my date. Do you have anything else in mind this evening?"

"I thought we might get acquainted and take it from there. I have an exciting idea or two but that is my surprise for the evening."

"Now you have my curiosity worked up. What kind of surprise?"

Charles teased, "It would be better if we got into that after dinner. Let's order something to eat first."

When the waiter re-appeared, Charles ordered peppered halibut over alder charcoal, and Janet selected her favorite, baked wild salmon balsamic on cedar wood.

"Charles, can't you tell me your surprise while we are waiting for dinner? You know I can't be patient until afterward. Please!"

"Well, OK. I'm not very good at keeping secrets anyhow, and we can discuss the details after we eat. So, what will you be doing on October eleventh?"

"Oh, the eleventh? I am going to be spending our first wedding anniversary with my wonderful husband. Actually, I haven't yet planned anything special. And what will you be doing?"

"Do you remember telling me about how thrilled you were as a little girl taking train rides from Chicago with your folks? You have often mentioned a favorite desire to take another train ride. So, I have put one together, and I needed to tell you about it in advance so that you can get a few days off work. Four days is all I can spare from my office, but here it is."

"Oh, Charlie!" she squealed. "Have you fixed us up with a real train ride?"

"Yep, I think it will be a real experience, and we will again be seeing some of the countryside that we truly love and have never forgotten. We fly from here to Billings on the afternoon of October 10 and stay the night at the Enchantment Lodge. The next morning we board the Silver Empire streamliner and travel to Bozeman for a bus trip into Yellowstone for our anniversary.

Afterward, we stay the night on the train until early morning to take new travelers aboard. We then ride down the Gallatin Valley to Butte and then to Missoula on the twelfth. The train has everything; private compartments, porters, vista dome lounges and a dining car. We stay the final night at a nice motel in Missoula and fly back here on the thirteenth. Just think, no phones or interruptions, just a couple days of real relaxation and enjoyment. What does my bride think about that little anniversary plan?"

"Charlie, that is a dream come true! I will treasure our trip for the rest of my life. I am so excited I don't know what to say except, 'thank you, Charlie, I love you!'"

"Wow! I sure didn't run into many obstacles selling that venture!"

They talked about the trip until dinner arrived and continued for an hour afterward.

"Charlie, I can't wait to get started. That will be a wonderful few days and surely there are train rides like that in other places. What if I want to do that every anniversary?"

"Janet, if that is what you want, then that is just what we'll do."

CHAPTER 23

Metamorphosis

The Silver Empire tour train.

Ben Andrews, Justice Brigade treasurer, had now become the organization's purser for a very special mission. In a very tight time frame, he had to make up seven packets containing very special identity cards with $50,000 in cash in each. Ten tourist train tickets completed the paperwork with one of four "helpers" boarding in Billings, two in Bozeman and one in Butte. But more materials were needed for the upcoming "theatricals." He dared not buy all the required costuming and props in Butte, out of concern for creating an investigative trail, and late in the morning made his way to other communities east of Butte. In a Whitehall general store, he found twelve yards of black muslin and fifty safety pins which would all do nicely to create seven Catholic nun outfits. An office stapler would be used to complete the "seamstress" work.

After that stop, he drove on Interstate 90 to a Bozeman mall and found a hobby store that fortunately had one of his necessities in stock. He bought two sets of six inch black vinyl stick-on letters that would spell out "SAINT REMUS SCHOOL", although there was no "Saint Remus School" in Montana that he knew of. As expected, the checkout clerk routinely flipped the packets through the scanner without noticing the letters he had selected.

A few doors away Ben found a paint and wallpaper store. He began searching for adhesive-backed wall paper of a special solid yellow color. As near as possible, it had to be school bus yellow and, ideally, would be ten inches wide and eight feet long. But he knew that all of those specifications together would be impossible to find. He soon observed that there was no solid yellow wall paper of any kind on hand. He browsed around and declined offers of help from a clerk who hovered nearby. Then he found it. The shelf paper was a bit brighter shade of yellow than he preferred and twelve inches wide. It was not an exact fit but one that would be unnoticed at a distance. Within minutes, he was checked out and driving back to Butte. On his way, he made a call to Henry Lowell on his cell phone.

"Hello Henry. Uh, thinking about that vehicle we talked about the other day, can it be available the night before so that we can add a couple of details to it?"

"Sure can, Ben, just drop over at your convenience. I will have it in my barn."

"Good enough. Thanks, Henry." Ben was then on his way to make the rounds of banks and teller machines to collect the remainder of the cash he needed for the packets. He had already received the identification documents from a member of the U.S. Marshall Service and six tickets on the Silver Empire were in his desk.

On his way home that evening, he again dialed his cell phone to contact the voice mail of Captain Harold Miller. "Hello Harold, this is Ben. I just wanted to let you know that my checklist is complete." It was the morning of October 10th when Harold Miller relayed the remainder of his "tasks completed" messages to Charles Gettys' voice mail. He and Janet were busy packing for their flight to Billings and a memorable trip on the Silver Empire.

On October 11, a bright, crisp Montana morning found Lieutenant John Lake of the Kalispell police and Sid Baker of the Border Patrol checking out a commuter jet parked at the Bigfork airport. "John, if you can get her fueled up sometime today, I will have this bird started up and on her way at daybreak."

"That's just what we need, Sid. Let's go over the plan again. You make no identity calls for clearances from anyone and if you have to, fake it. From here, you take a course to Butte and park on the fringe of the non-commercials to wait for a highway patrolman escorting a lady out onto the tarmac. His name is Dan Davis. It should be somewhere around 9:30 A.M. You take her aboard, crank up and fly east to River Port, South Dakota. As soon as she is in the company of those who will greet her there, you take off and head west to the mountain area I have marked on the map, out in the mountains north of Riggins, Idaho.

"Out there you will be met by an old retired friend, Vinegar Bill. He owns a ranch on an old, patented mining claim which is a packing and outfitting station for elk hunting guides in Idaho. He flies his own Cessna and has a bull dozer and some heavy equipment, which he occasionally uses for gold prospecting. Bill will be waiting for you and will probably want to drown you with coffee and talk your leg off. His dear wife died three years ago of cancer so he is a lonely old bachelor."

"I won't mind that a bit, but will he get me back to Eureka at a decent hour?" asked Baker. "I have Friday off, but am assigned to backup duty this weekend. Also, I want to point out that flying this jet rig is like joining Star Trek for a Cessna pilot. Is he checked out to use a bird like this?"

"Sid, I think it is safe to say that this plane will vanish out there, never to be seen again and he won't have use of it. You can be sure that old Vinegar will get you safely back to Eureka in his Cessna for evening dinner with the wife. I trust this will be one of the most forgettable days in your life."

Baker nodded in agreement. They completed a final check of the aircraft and made their way back to the patrol cruiser. After Lake dropped Baker off at the Border Patrol office in Eureka, he picked up his cell phone and called Harold Miller. He reported to the call recorder, "Harold, this is John. It is 09:25 P.M. on Thursday and all is set in Bigfork for tomorrow."

Early in the week, the Silver Bow sheriff had arranged for two of his jailers to have a liaison conference with correction officers at the Deer Lodge Prison on Friday, October 12. It was a concocted, but realistic and convenient way for them to be elsewhere. With the two deputies who were JB members, he privately went over their instructions.

"Guys, tomorrow is the big day. Our seven prisoners must be brought out of the jail, fed and escorted over to the judge at 0900. At about 15 minutes before then, you will be "immobilized" by bandits who will come in here to put our folks into costumes. I suggest you do whatever is necessary to make sure you have some kind of lumps or wounds on your heads to make the incident realistic. You aren't going to be witnesses to anything other than being 'assaulted.'

"When the parties are properly dressed, they will go on their own out to a little school bus and quickly disappear. At some later time, let's say about 0920 or so, you wake up and stagger into this office to raise the escape alarm with me and the city police. You also advise the judge. You are not yet fully coherent and have no details to offer anyone. I will call the Highway Patrol and the FBI to get them moving on blockades and all that stuff.

"The day after, we will begin secretly going after all the evidence on the case that we have stored here and will have to do a 'black bag' on anything the clerk has."

The U.S. Attorney's files will have already been gathered. Everything we grab will be transported to my ranch where I have a burn trench prepared. Within a few days, it will all be turned into smoke and ashes, and the trench bull-dozed over.

"Make no mistake, boys, this will go down as possibly the biggest jailbreak in U.S. history. It is going to be intense and hot as hell for all of us for a long time to come. If you don't think you can handle it and want to step aside, say so right now and nothing will be said." Neither of the men declined.

"Sheriff, speaking for myself, I feel that what we are going to do is a piece of real justice for good and loyal folks. They don't deserve to be prosecuted for taking big risks in the name of Montana law and order. They were out to get rid of real criminals in ways we once called heroic. To treat them as criminals now is not what real justice means. I am signed on for the whole shebang."

"I feel just the same, sheriff," said the other deputy.

"Ok then, we are all set for this big roller-coaster. I will see you early in the morning." The deputies made their way to the office door as the sheriff made his call to Harold Miller who had been mentally rehearsing his role in the following morning's events. He would make sure that Dan Davis would be in his cruiser at 0900 in the morning, close by the courthouse but out of sight, to await the arrival of former U.S. Attorney, Anita Martin.

Miller would be available for the emergency call from the Sheriff about the escape and immediately dispatch his officers to roadblocks on every highway route out of the Butte area. He would then make contact with the FBI to set up and take charge of a command center. They would have to call upon authorities in the U.S. Forest Service to man outposts on all forest roads in the area. Everything must be done to make this an effective, flawless pursuit of the fugitives, and it would continue for as long as necessary. Lots of long, hard hours lay ahead for Captain Harold Miller of the Montana Highway Patrol.

Thursday passed all too quickly for Ben Andrews and the sun was setting behind the mountains as he made his way to the ranch of Henry Lowell's friend, a local school bus driver. A barking dog announced his arrival beside the farm house and Henry came out to meet him. "Hi, Henry. I'll park over by the barn so that we can unload some of the stuff I have here."

Within minutes, the contents of his car were unloaded and arrayed inside the barn beside a medium size yellow school bus. "We can use jack knives or scissors on this shelf paper here," he advised Lowell. We want to cut it to fill in the yellow background where the name of the bus is. Once we get it stuck up, I have a new name we can lay on it, "St. Remus School."

"St. Remus School? Where in hell is that?" Lowell scoffed.

"Well, it sure as hell ain't in Montana. And the real fun will start when I see how you do some dress cutting and seamstress work here."

"Dress cutting? We are going to make dresses here? Are you nuts?"

"Nope, we are going to make us seven nun outfits right here. I got some black muslin, old bed sheets and some cardboard and that is what we are gonna do." As they worked trimming and placing the yellow shelf paper onto the proper locations on the bus, Andrews continued, "We are not going to make anything fancy but it has to look realistic. We can use glue, staples and safety pins, and we are going to have seven nun rigs for tomorrow's big stage play."

With the yellow shelf paper trimmed and in place, they moved to carefully positioning the black vinyl letters. In a few minutes the bus would bear the identity of St. Remus School. Andrews went on, "I will park by the station and walk over to join you at the courthouse. On the way, I will drop Anita's packet off with Patrolman Davis who will be parked near the courthouse. By a quarter to nine, our subjects should all be in a central holding room. I will wait on the bus while you take their outfits into the jail with you. Tell the players to help each other dress out as nuns and calmly walk out to the bus.

"Once they get into the bus, they take the outfits off and dress in the tourist clothes I have gathered up for them. While we drive them over to the station, I hand out their packets and give them last minute instructions. They each have a card inside telling them their destinations. We dump them off, come back here, take down the signs and burn them up along with the costumes and envelopes. I hope I have thought of most everything."

"Yep," Lowell replied, "Sounds to me like you've covered it pretty well. I can't see how anything can go wrong with our part, but there sure are lots of little chores spread out in this plan that all need to come together perfectly. Do you think it will work out?"

"I know it can work, Henry, aside from errors and accidents. We just have to remember the details and we will pull off a masterpiece!"

Time passed quickly as they worked on the costumes under the dim lights of the barn and shop. Bundles of clothing and shoes were carefully placed on seats, and Anderson wrote names on pieces of masking tape which were carefully placed on the seat backs. When they finished, the time of their final commitment was less than twelve hours away. Andrews joined Lowell with his friend and his wife in the farmhouse kitchen for late coffee and general conversation. It was a welcomed respite for what Andrews knew would be a very nervous, sleepless night. On his way home, he called in a report to Harold Miller.

During the time Anderson spent chatting with the Lowells, Charles and Janet Gettys were enjoying a late dinner in the Enchantment Lodge in Billings. "We can sleep late in the morning, Janet. The train won't arrive until about noon, and I know we are in for a great adventure. We'll be stopping tomorrow in the Bozeman area for the trip out to Yellowstone and back in the evening. There will be dinner on the town and sleep in our compartment for the final leg down to Missoula in the morning."

"This is so very romantic, Charles, and truly exciting for me."

"I fully share your excitement. You have no idea," he grinned.

On Friday, October 12, the shadows slowly receded from the hills and valleys of Butte, Montana, as a brilliant morning sun rose above the surrounding mountains. After an overnight pause in Bozeman, a few hours to the east of Butte, the Silver Empire was tracing steel rails through ghostlike mists that hovered over rippling streams. The train would arrive in Butte at exactly 08:50 and would board new passengers there and depart at 09:30, with its next stop at Missoula. As the silver train smoothly devoured the rails, some of the passengers were quietly enjoying breakfast and coffee amid magnificent views of mountainous western Montana.

Far northward, the two-engine executive jet, formerly owned by the late Jeep Rodgers, made its way to the take-off position at the end of the Bigfork airport single runway. In minutes, it was off the ground, climbing in a turn to the southeast and a direct heading to Butte. The aircraft was handling very well and all systems were properly functioning. After engaging the auto pilot, Sid Baker stretched and fell into amused and excited emotions about his mission. The Justice Brigade had called on him and that was a great honor. He knew nothing of the overall plan, but had strong feelings that it was something big. It could never eclipse the national notoriety of the recent federal bust of the JB vigilante bunch, but might come close. His excitement kept him finely attuned to carrying out each of the three elements he was responsible for, and he hoped that someday he would learn how his role fit into the entire project.

Highway Patrolman Dan Davis was in his cruiser early after a sleepless night. Through several cups of coffee, he watched the minutes tick away at a truck stop cafe. At 08:30 he was on his way to a position near the Silver Bow County Courthouse where he could park and not be conspicuous. He had covered the area many times before picking the right place, and he now drove directly to it. He was there by 08:45. Davis knew only that his assignment was part of a much greater plan, and he was impatient to get it over with. He too was excitedly contemplating what would be revealed about the entire scheme in days to come.

Shortly after Patrolman Davis was on station, a yellow school bus from St. Remus School eased to park at the curb along the west side of the courthouse. At almost the same instant, Davis was approached by Ben Andrews who gave a rap on his window. "Hey Ben! How are you this fine morning?"

"Doing great, Dan. I have a little packet here for you to give to Anita. She will be joining you in a few minutes, dressed as a nun. Give her our instructions once she is with you and have her change into the clothes I have in this little bag. Have a nice trip to the airport and find a good place to burn up whatever is left behind."

"Well," Davis replied, "it looks like this will be a day for the books and a great day for flying." He chuckled, "Anita should have a good flight under way before all hell breaks loose!"

"Yep, friend, this day will soon be known from here to Mongolia, and we will never even be able to tell our grandchildren about it. Have a good ride and I will catch you later." Andrews ambled off toward the parked school bus in time to see Henry Lowell step out to wait for him with a large trash bag in hand.

"Hey! Where in hell is St. Remus School, huh?"

On his way up the steps of the courthouse, Lowell called back with a wide grin, "Rock and roll! You seen any nuns around here?"

Ben stepped aboard the bus, chuckled and waved him on. For the umpteenth time, he counted the remaining packets and bundles of clothing. Yes, six units of each. Minutes later, in the distance he heard the deep blast of a train horn as it cleared the crossing near the Butte station. "I guess that would be the Silver Empire, right on time," he mused to himself. "Seems like that train called Lowell right back out of the courthouse."

Lowell appeared on the courthouse steps and walked quickly to the bus. Without speaking, he took his place in the driver's seat and started the engine. He nervously caught Ben's eye in the rear-view mirror, gave the "thumbs up" sign and smiled. In less than another minute, a single nun descended the same steps at the side of the courthouse and hurriedly made her way toward the parked Highway Patrol cruiser. As soon as she was inside, it was on its way and quickly out of view.

Three minutes after the cruiser disappeared, the side door of the courthouse again opened and a single file of six hefty nuns began descending the steps. Inconspicuously, they walked to the little bus and quietly settled themselves inside, yet they were breathing hard and all were speechless. Instantly, the doors closed and the bus was in motion. Standing in the little aisle, Andrews greeted them, "Hello ladies! You look like you have had a real rough night. You haven't been drinkin' and foolin' around with guys, have you?"

A gruff male voice responded, "Hell yes we have! And you're looking like fair game yourself Anderson!" everyone cheered.

"We have only a few minutes in here so get out of those outfits and change into the street clothes and shoes you'll find laid out on the seats. I bummed a lot of them from your kinfolks and got your sizes for the extra stuff I bought. You each have a new shaving kit with toiletries. Your names are on pieces of masking tape on the seat backs. Go for it!"

Fumbling, cursing, laughing and straining, they hurriedly changed clothes. Tensions began to vanish and sighs of relief filled the interior of the vehicle as the bus approached the Butte railroad station. "OK, here's the last word guys," said Anderson. "I will go through your real names to call out a packet for each of you. You will open it, remove the contents and give the envelope back to me. Inside you will find new ID's. They are complete, legal ID documents. That is the new you! Memorize your names. Introduce yourselves to each other and never use your real names again! The former 'you' no longer exists.

"We have made preparations for your families to join you under your new identities . . . . and theirs! That will naturally take some time and cannot all happen at once. Trust that you are not going to be isolated for long so just focus on making your new ID work, wherever you land.

"You will board the train as tourists for the pleasure ride from here to Pasco, Washington. You are all assigned to the first Pullman car behind the vista dome and must remain there. If anyone asks about luggage, tell them it was already checked aboard. You have private compartments, and I want to warn you again not to venture out of them for the whole trip to Pasco. Someone from the JB will advise where each of you will depart the train between here and there, who will meet you, and how and when your families may be able to join you.

"This will probably go down as the largest jailbreak in U.S. history so the lid of secrecy is now on . . . FOREVER! It's gonna be red hot in Montana for some time to come. The JB is proud of you and you will soon learn that it thrives in places far beyond Montana's borders. All of us will miss you and think of you often. Maybe we will find a way to get together from time to time. Good luck to each of you!"

Lowell brought the bus to a stop in the parking lot beyond the entrance to the station. Six well-dressed passengers dismounted and found their way to the Pullman car behind the vista dome lounge and were met for a check of their tickets by the conductor. They were comfortably settled into their compartments when the train began to move. Lowell and Anderson were then on their way in the bus to attend to the last details of their part in the plan.

Janet barely roused from her sleep when the train stopped in Butte, but Charles had been up for over an hour, mentally struggling with everything that could go wrong at this critical juncture in the JB plans they had so quickly pieced together. His sleep had been brief and restless. He greeted Janet with a kiss on the cheek and asked her to enjoy her slumber. "A hot latte is on the way for you and I am going to the lounge car to see if I recognize any of our new travelers. I will be back in a few minutes and we will go forward for a nice breakfast." Janet mumbled a reply and went back to sleep.

Charles quietly closed the metal compartment door and made his way to the vista dome where he quickly caught the eye of middle-aged Ginny Decker, police chief of Sunrise City, seated alone at a lounge table. In a casual wave, she greeted him with a touch of three fingers to her right brow and he took a seat beside her. Breathlessly, he asked, "Has anything gone wrong?"

She grinned in reply, "What ever could you mean by that Charles? Of course, everything has gone exactly according to plan and all of our little mates are safely on board, one flying off to a secret place." She softly chuckled, "Did you expect anything else?"

He gasped a deep sigh of relief and said, "Do you mean that with all those little details, we actually pulled it off? Wow! I haven't slept for days! Ok, so what is next?"

"Well, shame on you for under-rating us! I have here in this heavy brief case all they will need for the last part of this journey. One goes all the way to Pasco and the others get off from Missoula to Thompson Falls and Sand Point.

I have set it up to have them met by escorts to their final destinations. Piece of cake! Uhh . . . you look like you need a drink."

Twenty minutes later, the Silver Empire was up to speed, glistening in the fresh sunlight as it slipped through the towns of Anaconda and Warm Springs. It smoothly increased the distance between itself and a scene behind it of alarm and chaos in the city of Butte, Montana. An inconceivable jail break had occurred at some time around 09:00 that morning. Seven desperate federal fugitives were on the loose, and the authorities were issuing commands and orders to every level of law enforcement to intercept them at all conceivable points of egress from Butte. An infinite net of law enforcement was being cast to catch them. But the passengers on the Silver Empire were unaware of it all. While they relaxed, a small executive jet with a pilot and one passenger had reached altitude and set a course from Butte to River Port, South Dakota.

The first official responses to the emergency fell like a deluge upon Captain Harold Miller of the Montana Highway Patrol. He immediately made contact with the FBI field office, and they agreed to set up a command post in Miller's office on the outskirts of Butte. The first one to join Miller there was the Silver Bow County Sheriff. The FBI Special Agent-In-Charge, James Holcomb, arrived within minutes to take charge of the situation and gather input for positioning road blocks. As each point was defined on the large, plastic-covered wall map, officers were dispatched to where they would remain until relieved. Their positions were identified with colored marking pens as they checked in. Soon the command post was joined by the Butte Chief of Police and the Deputy Commander of Confinement at the Deer Lodge Prison. Communication levels were delegated and all off-duty personnel were summoned into service.

When the planned responses began to take shape on the map, the hastily formed command staff entered into discussion and debate on strategies. Each had his own version of "most likely" disposition of the fugitives and the Sheriff was first to explain his. "Guys, these are highly trained and experienced law enforcement people we are after here. They were some of our best, and I think they have the help of the Justice Brigade on the whole deal. They know exactly what our responses will be and will do just the opposite to thwart us. With roadblocks out all over hell, my best bet is that they will go to ground immediately and stay put until the up-front force is pulled back. They may have walked only a couple of blocks to get into a hideout or whatever."

The Butte Police Chief spoke next. "Roy, I agree with that estimate and will work with my commanders to grid out the city from the courthouse outward and cover every block looking for witnesses or suspicious persons. That said my guess is that they would get away from Butte as soon as possible before the heat comes on. We have no witnesses on exactly when or how they got away. I think there was

JB transportation waiting someplace and that they were taken out over the mountain roads that nobody looks at. We have hundreds of miles of such trails all around us."

Holcomb responded, "Yes, that's the reason why I alerted the District Rangers of the two forests here to dispatch their people for surveillance at all critical points. They will be joining us here soon."

Miller added his viewpoint, "Our roadblocks on major intersections will have a calming effect on the public as well as a real purpose. In my mind, those guys would want to get out of Butte ahead of any moves on our part to surround them, and I think they may have had time to do it. They possibly headed up either Interstate 90 or Interstate 5 and are going like hell away from here. They know our next jump would be to jurisdictions down the line so I expect them to have a ranch or camp to hole up in out there in the big, wide, empty world of Montana. That would be very hard to cover . . . will take a long time."

Nods and comments signified agreement around the conference room. As the mechanics and deliberations of their work continued, the press descended upon them and word arrived that the governor would be visiting the command center sometime in the afternoon. Focus on apprehension of the fugitives was interrupted in order to deal with keeping people informed and managing the political scenario. It would be hours before an incidental discovery by the Butte Federal Clerk of Court would raise a new and alarming complexity that everyone agreed to keep strictly confidential. To the ones who knew the details, it was a disaster!

In preparing for the court appearance of the accused, the federal court clerk had gathered a number of documents required by the judge. When he became aware of the escape, he collected the documents and went to place them back into their respective case files. But the case files were gone! Everything was gone! Copies of arrest records, news clippings, individual mug shots, fingerprint cards, depositions, witness statements . . . all had disappeared!

In a panic, he called the prosecuting attorney, sheriff's office and police headquarters. As soon as they were able to check their files, the same report came back. Nothing was there! The U.S. attorney called to the forensic lab in Missoula to make sure that bones and tissue samples collected from the Snowshoe mine shaft were protected. Too late! Everything had already disappeared! His urgent call to the Sheriff's office received the same reply. Investigation notes, computer disks, and all items of physical evidence in the secured case locker had been cleaned out. No one knew how or when the thefts had occurred.

If the fugitives were ever caught, how would law enforcement be able to prosecute them without evidence? It would solely depend on the cooperation of their key witness, Reamy Nelson, living in Utah under an assumed identity in the witness protection program. Weeks later, as they tried to re-assemble the pieces of the case, the authorities would discover that Nelson had complete memory loss about his involvement with the Justice Brigade and could not be convinced to reveal anything. With fugitives still at large, he had every reason to avoid further exposure.

But as the day of the escape continued, the Silver Empire gracefully wound its way down the Deer Lodge valley. Six very relieved tourists anxiously watched the peaceful scene slip by outside their windows. After enjoying breakfast, Brigham Johnson and Tom Nash shared a compartment. Outside they could see flashing police cruiser lights massed at the highway interchange near Garrison. "Well, Tom, it looks like law enforcement has planned a little party for someone," he chuckled. "I wonder who that might be."

Tom answered with a laugh, "Must be some low life who slipped out of custody. Folks will have to watch out for blood-thirsty criminals on the loose around here!"

Out of Butte, the train continued its leisurely pace down the Deer Lodge Valley as Charles and Janet Gettys were finishing a late breakfast. In the next hour they would be on the station platform in Missoula for a cab ride to the airport for their return flight to Olympia. On the trip, Charles had intentionally failed to turn his cell phone on and neither of them had seen the live, televised news announcements of the prison escape. They were blissfully out of contact and excited about their little tourist adventure.

In the Butte command center, roadblock dispatches were nearing completion as surveillance reports began to filter in. None of the positioned officers had contacts to report.

The press was in a frenzy of demands. Logs of citizen reports of fugitive sightings began to grow, and each report required the immediate response of an officer to check it out. Police resources began to dwindle. It would be a long day, an even longer week, and the future would hold no promises that their mission would ever be achieved successfully. Morale among the officials manning the command center was marginal at best but no one spoke of the dismal feelings they were experiencing. A personal visit from retiring Governor Harold Smith brought little comfort to its strained workers.

In the distance, four loud blasts of the Silver Empire's horn announced its approach to the Rattlesnake Creek crossing, minutes away from the Missoula station. Charles and Janet took their places at the exit along with other passengers detraining there. The train rolled smoothly into the siding and came to rest at the old Northern Pacific station. Doors opened, uniformed train workers stepped down and stood to assist passengers onto the platform. When the way was clear, Charles brought their luggage forward behind two other travelers who began boarding for the continuation run of the Silver Empire to Pasco, Washington. As Charles stepped down, he was immediately greeted by the familiar face of a friend who had come to see other Missoula travelers off at the station.

With a casual salute of three fingers to the brow, the man smiled and said, "Greetings brother, nice to see you here!" Charles returned the touch to his brow with three fingers.

There it was, the introductory symbol, "three". He reached out to grasp the man's hand in a strong handshake with his right hand and clasped two fingers of his left hand over them. The other did the same. It was an exchange of five fingers clasped, covered by two fingers of the other hand, representing the number "seven". The hands were pumped three times and parted. Three "sevens" were thereby passed between them, creating an old, secret greeting that could never be detected by the uninformed, the recognition code of the Montana vigilantes, 3-7-77.

"How was your trip, Charles?"

"It was a wonderful ride, Gregory; everything is perfect, to the last detail. Let me introduce you to my wife. Janet, this is one of my old friends, Gregory Martin, the man who is campaigning for the November election to replace Harold Smith. He will be the next governor of Montana."